THE TRIDENT SERIES

DIEGO

Book 8

Jaime Lewis

This is a work of fiction. Names, characters, businesses, events, and incidents are the products of the author's imagination. Any resemblance to actual persons, living or dead, or actual events is purely coincidental.

The Trident Series - Diego
Copyright © 2021 by Jaime Lewis

All rights reserved. No part of this book may be reproduced or transmitted in any form or by any means without written permission from the author.

ISBN: 978-1-952734-22-9

TABLE OF CONTENTS

Chapter 1	1
Chapter 2	3
Chapter 3	11
Chapter 4	18
Chapter 5	23
Chapter 6	37
Chapter 7	47
Chapter 8	52
Chapter 9	56
Chapter 10	62
Chapter 11	69
Chapter 12	83
Chapter 13	93
Chapter 14	96
Chapter 15	103
Chapter 16	113
Chapter 17	122
Chapter 18	125
Chapter 19	137
Chapter 20	149
Chapter 21	160
Chapter 22	167
Chapter 23	175
Chapter 24	177
Chapter 25	184
Epilogue	187

CHAPTER ONE

Mitchell Langford stared at the glass in front of him, half-filled with Jack and Coke. His fingers itched to wrap around the cold drink as his taste buds begged for just a tiny sample of the whiskey inside.

Every night for the last year, he fought the urge to give in and satisfy his craving. It had been too long since he had a drop of alcohol, not since the night that Belle informed him that she was considering moving to New York to pursue her dancing career. That night hadn't ended well for her nor himself, for that matter. She had pushed him too far on a night she had been warned to leave him alone, and it resulted in her unleashing the monster that lived within him.

Not only had he destroyed her dancing career, but he nearly destroyed everything he had worked for. He should be in prison for assault, battery, rape, and probably a slew of other charges. Surprisingly, Campbell refused to press charges, and she lied, telling the hospital that she had broken her leg when she tripped and fell down the stairs. Who knows, maybe she was delirious from the pain she was in, or she knew better than to squeal on him.

Before she was released from the hospital after a several-week stay as she recovered from major surgery to repair the bones in her leg, she told him that she would only agree to come back if he agreed to stop drinking and change his ways. He happily obliged, knowing that things would eventually go back to the way they were, where he was in control.

She didn't have any other option but to come back with him. After her old man died two years ago, she didn't have a pot to piss in because her dad supported her while she went to college and pursued dancing.

Campbell had been an astounding ballet dancer, filled with poise, grace, and elegance. If he hadn't taken a baseball bat to her leg, she most likely would be the star dancer of some famous ballet company.

All she had to do was walk into a room, and Mitchell's body would react in a way it never did with any other woman. He was turned on by her demeanor, personality, and most importantly, her beauty. She was petite and had gorgeous long strawberry blonde hair that he loved raking his fingers through, especially when she was in his bed. He missed her in his bed. But that was something he had to deal with, because the other half of their agreement after she was released from the hospital to resume her recovery at home was that she would be allowed to move back into the guest house.

He paid for everything; the medical bills, all her essentials, and anything else she needed. All she had to her name was the old piece of junk truck that had belonged to her dad, and whatever small amount of money she made in tips at the lame job she had at the diner in town. Soon he'd see to it that she quit that job and start concentrating on what it entailed to be his wife. Because soon she was going to marry him whether she liked it or not. He had already sacrificed so much for them to be together, including murder.

Mitchell took another look at the glass. It taunted him, but he had made it this far without giving in; another few days wasn't going to kill him.

CHAPTER TWO

Fred Wilson, a former U.S. Navy SEAL turned diner owner, watched Belle, one of his waitresses, as she delivered another tray of food to one of the tables. She favored her left leg, which wasn't a surprise, but it seemed to be bothering her more than usual today. Ever since she returned to work after her so-called accident, he kept on her about not overdoing it. She was a stubborn girl, but damn if she hadn't found a way into his and his wife's hearts. Both he and Stella had taken an instant liking to her when she first came into the diner four years ago and applied for a job. She had made such a great first impression that Stella hired her on the spot. Since then, she'd been his number one employee, and a daughter that he and Stella had always wanted but never had. Even more so with the unexpected passing of her father two years ago.

Being a former SEAL, Fred had a knack for reading people. It came in handy throughout his career and even in his personal life, especially about six months after Belle's dad was killed in a freak accident. That was when she started getting involved with Mitchell Langford, the man who owned the company her dad worked for.

You could always count on Belle's smile to light up a room, but after she started seeing Mitchell, all of that changed. She wasn't the bright and cheerful woman she once was. But he'd give her credit for trying, though he saw right through her façade.

It pissed Fred off when Mitchell had taken advantage of a grieving young woman who didn't have any financial backing except for what she made at the diner. He and Stella had offered her assistance until she could get on her feet, but it had been too late. Mitchell had already charmed her and sucked her into his web of lies and corruption.

Mitchell Langford had a bad reputation in town, but he had the right people in his back pocket. That was in part of his financial stability. Even the Sherriff couldn't touch him. If he did, the local prosecuting attorney would drop whatever charge was brought against him. He knew that was the reason why Belle never pressed any charges against him when she ended up in the hospital battered and broken. Hell, nobody dared to cross him because they feared retaliation. Fred would love to put the little pussy in his place, and he could if he wanted to, but again, like others, he feared the blowback. He would never endanger his wife. That wasn't saying that down the road, he couldn't make the man disappear, because after all, that had been part of his job years ago. He and his team made many bad and corrupt people disappear, and he wouldn't hesitate to perform a Houdini act on Mitchell Langford.

Belle approached the counter where he stood. Again, he saw the tightness in her slight smile and knew she was trying to hide the pain she was in.

"Belle, go back to the office and take a break." He told her in that deep, commanding voice of his.

She squinted her eyes at him. "I don't need a break." She countered, then took a step, but her leg gave out from under her. Thankfully she caught the bar stool next to her before she tumbled onto the floor.

Fred hurried around the counter and helped her stand upright. She was tiny compared to him. She tilted her head back to look up at him.

"Okay. Maybe I do need a break." She admitted, making him frown.

"I swear, you and Stella are the most stubborn women I know." He muttered under his breath as he helped her down the hall to his office.

Once he got her to a chair, he slid another chair over in front of her to prop her leg up. She leaned over and started to rub it. Every so often, he heard a small gasp come from her. She was definitely sore. But he could also see the fire in her eyes. She still held a lot of anger stemming from the accident. After all, it dashed any hope she had of escaping the small town to pursue her dancing.

Campbell knew Fred was upset. He had voiced his displeasure with her decision to be released from the hospital in Mitchell's care. She also knew Fred suspected that Mitchell was responsible for her injuries, but she had lied and told him and everyone else that she had tripped and fallen down the stairs. Telling the truth would only have caused her more pain, or possibly even death. Mitchell Langford wasn't a man to mess with. Unfortunately for her, she fell for his charm and words of promise. That had only lasted about six months, and then she began to see the real Mitchell Langford. He was verbally and physically abusive, and extremely controlling. There wasn't a damn thing she could do. She tried twice to leave him, and somehow, he had found her before she even made it out of town. She paid the price for her actions. There were times she really wanted to confide in Fred and Stella, but she refused to put them in the middle of her problems. They didn't need any trouble on her part.

She dug her thumbs into her flesh as she tried to rub out the pain. Fred was right; she had overdone it. But if she didn't work, she'd be stuck at home with Mitchell, which was the last place she wanted to be. She just needed a few more weeks, and she'd have enough money set aside to carry her until she could create a new life for herself somewhere far from the mountains of West Virginia and Mitchell Langford.

She pulled her pant leg up, exposing her mangled-looking leg. When Fred glanced at the deformed flesh, she pushed the material down, but it was too late. One look into his keen eyes, and she knew she had once again disappointed him.

"Belle..." He started to say, but she cut him off.

"Fred, please."

"I'm worried about you. And so is Stella. I know for a fact that you're covering for the son of a bitch. But the question I want to know is why?"

She took a deep breath.

"Fred, I respect you and Stella. I even consider you both family even though we aren't even related. And it is why I won't involve you in my situation with Mitchell. Plus, we both know that it's his word against mine, and right now, he has more friends on his side."

"I don't like it. You deserve so much better."

She smiled softly. "And one day, I'll have that. But for now, I have to play the game if I want to survive."

She didn't want to talk about it anymore because it would only lead to Fred getting more pissed off.

"I think I'll take your advice and call it a day. A nice hot bath with some Epsom Salts would do wonders for my muscles."

She stood, and so did Fred. Fred wasn't one to show his emotions much, so it had taken her by surprise when he pulled her into a hug. It was a much-needed hug. Her dad was a great hugger when she was feeling down. She missed him terribly.

Fred watched as Belle grabbed her purse and keys from behind the counter. Stella was talking to her, then hugged her before she left. He watched her the entire time as she hobbled to her truck.

He shook his head in disgust as he ran his hand down his face. He couldn't take it anymore. He knew she was scared to ask for help, and he couldn't blame her. Mitchell was a ruthless person who cared for nothing and nobody but himself, but he couldn't sit back and do nothing. He had to help her escape, and then a thought hit him. Hell, he didn't know why he hadn't thought of it before.

"I know that look of yours." He heard Stella say. When he turned his head, she stood there staring at him.

He smirked. "What look would that be?"

"You're up to something."

"I'm getting Belle the hell away from that asshole. Enough is enough. Every day I fear I'm going to get a call that he's killed her."

"What are you going to do? She's petrified of him. Look at the other times she's tried to run away from him. He beat her so bad she couldn't work for days."

He pulled his phone from his pocket. "I'm calling an old friend that I know will have some suggestions."

Derek Connors took a sip of his drink as he watched everyone enjoying themselves. Alex had once again outdone herself with the wedding decorations and set-up. He was happy for Dino and Skittles. They both married incredible women who complimented them. Although when he and his wife Juliette showed up for Dino and Arianna's wedding, they hadn't expected to see Skittles and Anna Grace standing at the alter with them. According to Alex, it was Arianna and Dino's idea to invite the other couple to share their wedding day.

It was hard to believe that two years ago, not one of his men on Alpha Team was even dating, and now, six of them were married, and one was engaged. The odd man out right now was Diego. But Derek knew it would only be a matter of time before a woman came along and captured Diego's heart.

He felt his phone vibrate and pulled it from his pocket. He didn't recognize the number. He excused himself from the party to take the call. As he walked into the house, he answered, "Hello?"

"Hey, Derek, Fred Wilson here."

Derek was surprised to hear the familiar voice. "Hey, Fred. How the hell are you? My god, it's been a while."

Derek's old SEAL buddy laughed. "Yeah, the wife keeps me busy nowadays."

"I bet. Do you and Stella still own that diner in West Virginia?"

"Sure do. But Stella is itching to move south. She's ready for some year-round warm weather."

"I can't blame her. Tell her I said hi." There was a slight pause, and Derek knew his friend called for a reason. "Well, I know you didn't call me out of the blue just to shoot the shit."

Fred sighed. "Yeah, I'm calling because I need some help. Well, not me exactly, but one of my employees."

Derek sensed the frustration in Fred's tone. He knew Fred would only be calling for help if it was really bad.

"What kind of help are we talking about?"

"I need to get her relocated."

"Shit. She? What kind of trouble is she in?"

"She's young and a hard worker, but dammit, I can't take seeing her coming to work bruised because some rich asshole thinks he can control her by manipulating and pounding on her."

Derek was quiet for a minute. That kind of shit upset him. Before he would agree to help, he needed clarification on some things. This woman may not want out of the relationship.

"What's her relationship with this guy?"

"There really isn't one. She's being forced to stay with him."

"Why doesn't she just leave him?"

"She's tried Derek, and each time she ended up in the hospital. And, before you ask, she's too scared to press charges. The sheriff in town knows the guy is an asshole, but his hands are tied if she won't press charges. Plus, the guy has a lot of people in his back pocket, including the district attorney. I need a way to sneak her out of town and stay hidden for a while. At least to see if his interest in her fades."

"What are you thinking?"

"I was hoping between you and Tink, with his connections, that you guys may have some suggestions. My hands are tied here as well, or I would up and leave town and take her with me."

Derek thought hard. Surely Tink could provide some options, but this young woman sounded like she was important to Fred, and Derek thought it might be best to keep her close by.

He scanned the area, not sure what he was looking for, but then he landed on Diego and smiled.

"Fred, I think I may have an idea. Let me talk to some people, and I'll give you a call in a couple of days. Hopefully, we can help this woman out."

Derek heard the relief in Fred's voice. "Thanks, Derek. I'll be awaiting your call."

"Talk to you later."

Derek hung up and took a drink from his bottle.

"What's going on?" Tink asked from behind him. Derek knew his buddy had walked into the room.

He turned around and faced him. "That was Fred Wilson."

Tink furrowed his eyebrows. "Fred? What's he up to?"

Derek grinned. "He's still in West Virginia, but Stella's driving him nuts about moving south."

Tink smiled. "I always liked her. I think she was the only woman who could put up with Fred's bad attitude."

"I think you're right."

"But I know that he didn't just call to say hi and tell you that Stella wants to move."

Derek chuckled. "No. He actually called asking for a favor. I wanted to run it by you as well, since you're in the business of protecting."

Tink raised an eyebrow in question. Personal protection wasn't the only business that Tink's company dealt with. They were involved in a lot of unsanctioned government operations.

Derek explained everything that Fred told him.

"Damn. Do you think she wants to leave?"

"That was exactly my thought, but Fred seems to think if we can sneak her out and hide her somewhere for a while that the guy may lose interest in her. I don't know the whole story, but from the looks of things, the woman is definitely afraid of the guy."

Tink ran his hand over his jaw, and Derek knew the big man was deep in thought.

"Are you thinking of keeping her local?" Tink finally asked.

Derek nodded. "I'd like to, since it's a favor for Fred. That way, we can somewhat keep an eye on her ourselves."

"Shit. We just took on three contracts. I don't know if I have the manpower right now. It's possible in a few weeks that I could have someone available. But it seems like Fred needs something quick."

"I Understand. I got the team undergoing some training for the next few weeks that will keep them in town."

"What are you thinking?" Tink asked curiously.

"Diego's got that big house on all those acres that he's been fixing up. Not to mention he's got the property wired with security. You should know since your company installed it."

Tink's eyes widened. "You think he'll go for it?"

"Don't know. All I can do is ask. I don't know who else I could ask that I can trust not to broadcast her whereabouts. He has that EOD training tomorrow that the FBI is hosting. I'll talk to him afterward."

CHAPTER THREE

On any other given day, Diego would be ecstatic to take part in new explosive ordinance disposal training, but today wasn't one of those days. His training partner was some jackass from a SWAT team out of New York with an ego the size of the universe. He was one of those guys who thought they knew everything, even when it was something new being taught to them. None of them attending the joint training were familiar with the new device making an appearance across Asia.

The next exercise they were running through was a timed event involving live explosives to provide a realistic experience. Each group was placed into a blast safe room with an explosive device. Nobody except for the instructors knew which device was in each room. Some of them had the new device, while some were equipped with aging devices.

Diego, along with Zelinski, his training partner, were escorted to their room. Diego looked up at the number above the door and shook his head—number thirteen. That alone should've been the first warning that the exercise wasn't going to go as planned.

They both took a seat in the two chairs in front of the rectangular table. The device was covered with a sheet so that they couldn't see it. Sitting next to the device on the table was a bag of tools. Once they heard a signal blast of a horn, they would be allowed to uncover it and begin working to diffuse it. Before they went into the room, they were both fitted with protective gear; a pair of safety glasses, a pull-on armored vest that covered the groin area, and a helmet. They were told that the devices were not armed to their max potential, so a complete bomb suit was not required.

Diego studied the covered device, noting the shape of it under the covering. He ran through his head which devices could match it. He thought of three. One of them being the new device they were shown today. He looked over at his partner and wanted to slap him upside the head. Instead of focusing, he had his phone out checking his Instagram account—un-fucking-believable.

"Hey, Zelinski," he called over to the dipshit. When he looked up, Diego said, "Think you can put that away and keep it there for the next ten minutes, or maybe until we finish this exercise?"

The guy rolled his eyes, but at least he slipped the phone into his pocket. Diego hoped one of the two cameras he saw in the room was recording and picked that up.

Suddenly the horn blasted, signaling to them to begin. Diego realized quickly that the guy had minimal experience when it came to explosives. He watched in horror as Zelinski just ripped the sheet from the device. He held his breath when the corner of the material snagged a sharp edge of the metal where the bomb was connected. It had been a miracle that he hadn't detonated the device then.

As soon as the entire device was revealed, Diego could see they'd been one of the unlucky ones and had the new device. The device had a timer that read four minutes and thirty-six seconds.

"Ah fuck! Just our luck." The guy looked over Diego. "I hope you were paying attention earlier."

Diego looked away and rolled his eyes. He reached over, opened the bag of tools, and pulled out the Philips head screwdriver. He didn't have time for this shit. He made a note to discuss this guy with the instructors. Just from his interaction with the guy, he didn't deserve to be anywhere near an explosive device.

The device they were working with was a souped-up version of a previous model. The only difference was how the wires were connected inside and the colors.

Diego followed the black wire as he was instructed. He glanced at the clock. He was down to three minutes and forty-two seconds. *No pressure*, he thought to himself. Zelinski was more interested in what was in the bag of tools than the device. Whatever. It was probably best he didn't touch it.

Just as he saw where the yellow wire was spliced with the black wire, he knew where to cut. He asked Zelinski, who stood right next to him, to grab the cutters. Instead of just handing him the cutters, the asshat threw it to him. The problem was that the guy's aim was just as bad as his behavior.

Diego watched in slow motion as the cutters landed inside the device. Suddenly the clock went from three minutes to zero, and Diego knew that wasn't a good sign.

He grabbed Zelinski just as the device exploded. It may not have been armed to the full capacity of the real one, but it still had force behind it. Diego took the brunt of the blast wave as he threw himself in front of his partner.

When he landed on the floor, his ears were flooded with a god-awful ringing sensation. His head felt full, his vision was blurry, and he felt as if he kept going in and out of unconsciousness until the icky blackness took over entirely and pulled him under.

Derek and the rest of Alpha Team sat in the waiting room anxiously awaiting word from the doctors on Diego's condition. He never expected to get a phone call informing him that one of his men was injured during a routine training exercise.

From what the instructor told him that if it hadn't been for Diego's fast reflexes, both Diego and the asshole from New York would've been in far worse condition.

Once he had hung up, he quickly notified the others who were off doing their training exercises, and they all met at the hospital.

Derek could see the concern on the team members' faces.

Suddenly, the door swung open, and a doctor walked in. Since they were the only ones in the room, the doctor walked over to where they were. Derek stood, as did the rest of the team.

"I assume you're all here for Chief Petty Officer Mateo Rivera." The doctor said, and Derek stuck his hand out.

"Yes, Sir. I'm CPO Rivera's Commanding Officer. Commander Derek Connors."

The doctor shook his hand. "Nice to meet you, Commander. I'm Captain Evers, specialist in neurotrauma."

"So, how's my man?" Derek asked.

"He's fortunate that it wasn't worse. He has a borderline grade two/three concussion. He's experiencing double vision, ringing in the ears, some disorientation, and of course, a major headache. The good news is that the CT scans came back with no issues. I'd like to keep him overnight as a precaution, to make sure no other symptoms appear. We'll do another scan in the morning, and if it comes back clean, he'll be free to go, but with limited duty. And when I say limited duty, I mean limited."

"How long are we talking?" Derek asked. He was concerned because he knew that if Diego's symptoms didn't subside, it was possible he'd never get cleared for active duty again.

"It all depends on the progression of his recovery. I would say at least two to four weeks of no activity, then if he's feeling up to it, a gradual return from there."

Derek shook his hand again. "Thank you, Captain. Can we see him?"

"Absolutely. When I left to come out here, they were preparing to move him to a room. He'll be on the fourth floor. If you want to head up there, the nurses will help you locate his room."

"Thank you again."

"No need to thank me. The brunt of his recovery is going to be on him. I know how men like him are—he just needs to stay focused and not overdo it too quickly."

Derek grinned. "We'll all make sure he stays within his boundaries."

"If you have any follow-up questions, the nurses know how to get in touch with me. I'll be back by tomorrow morning to check on him."

Diego pulled the string to turn off the light hanging over him before he laid his head back on the pillow and threw his arm over his eyes. Any movement at all created a tidal wave of pain crashing through his head.

Now that he'd had time to process the incident, he was pissed even more. Zelinski had the nerve to laugh the incident off once the paramedics said he'd be okay. He had even joked about Diego taking the brunt of the blast. He wondered how the fucker was even allowed around explosives. Diego couldn't help but wonder the mess they'd be dealing with had that device been wired to do the damage it would in a real scenario. A slight shiver traveled down his spine. Maybe he'd rather not wonder about that, because if it were wired like the real thing, he wouldn't be lying in a hospital bed with just a concussion and a few stitches in his side. He'd be lying in a drawer in a morgue, probably in pieces. *Fuck that shit.*

The light knock on the door drew him back to the present, and he moved his arm so he could see who the hell it was. He wasn't in the mood for visitors. But then he saw Derek standing there looking concerned.

"Hey, Commander."

Derek stepped in, and Diego wasn't surprised to see the rest of the team file in.

"How ya feeling?" Derek asked, keeping his voice to a light whisper as if knowing the pain he was in.

Diego rubbed his head. "Like my brain is too small for my head."

Dino snorted. "I find that hard to believe. You've got the biggest head of anyone I know."

Diego chuckled, knowing his friend and teammate was only joking, but even laughing hurt like a motherfucker.

"You're such an asshole," Diego told him but then looked at Derek.

"Did Clark call you?"

Derek nodded. "He did. I'm not going to lie; it scared the living shit out of me."

"Scared me too, after the fact. Any word on Zelinski?"

Derek pressed his lips together tight. "He's doing a hell of a lot better than you are right now. But again, that's thanks to you. You took the brunt of the blast's repercussion."

"It feels like I did."

"Yeah, well, the fucker owes you his life."

"He'd been screwing around all day. It was only a matter of time before he hurt someone. I'm just thankful it happened at training and not a live mission where that device could've killed everyone in proximity."

"The good news is that he won't be endangering any colleagues for the time being. His superiors were notified of his irresponsible behavior, and he's been placed on administrative leave."

Shit. Diego knew the guy wouldn't be happy about that. But hopefully, the guy would learn from this. Don't fuck around with explosives, even in a controlled environment.

"The doctor said you're going to be sidelined for a few weeks."

Diego tightened his lips. "I know. He already told me. He also said there was a slight possibility that some of my symptoms won't go away."

Derek narrowed his eyes, and Diego knew that look. The commander couldn't stand negativity, especially coming from one of his men. But this was serious. How could someone who knew what was a stake not understand? There was a chance that he may not get cleared by the review board to return to active duty with his injury.

"Let's not focus on that. Let's take this step by step. The first step is getting you out of the hospital and back home so you can rest and let your body heal."

"This is going to suck," Diego muttered, but then Ace spoke up.

"That also means no working on your house either."

"And if I catch you, I'll send a plane ticket to your mom and have her come out and babysit you," Derek teased, but Diego knew his commander would do it. Diego loved his mom, but damn, she was worse than a drill instructor.

"That's just mean, Commander," Diego said, and Derek chuckled.

Diego got serious and looked at all his teammates. They weren't just teammates; they were also his brothers. Even though they each had families of their own, their little unit was also a family.

"Can you guys just promise to come and visit me? I'll go stir crazy being there by myself and not able to do a damn thing."

Before any of the guys could say anything, Derek cleared his throat.

"Actually, that's another thing I wanted to talk to you about. First, you don't have to stay at the house. You are allowed to come to the base and attend meetings. I've already cleared that. Second, depending on what you say, you may not have to stay at your house alone. And you could look at it as a side job until you get cleared."

Diego raised an eyebrow. "Side job? I thought I wasn't allowed to do anything?"

"Well, in this case, you really don't have to do anything physical."

"Go on."

Derek proceeded to tell him about the phone call he got from his friend. He took it all in and thought about it.

"And you trust this girl?"

"I trust Fred, and he wouldn't ask for help if he didn't believe her."

Diego closed his eyes. He trusted Derek and knew that Derek wouldn't ask him for this type of favor if it wasn't important. He opened his eyes and looked at Derek.

"I'll do it. What's the timeline?"

"We'll give you a few days to rest. Ace said he would drive you up to get her. Potter and Irish are going as well. Just in case this guy shows up and makes a scene."

"Sounds like a plan."

CHAPTER FOUR

Campbell toed her sneakers off and flung them into the oversized walk-in closet. She eyed over all of the designer clothes that lined the multiple racks. Over half of them still had the tags. They were all bought by Mitchell. He tended to want to dress her when he threw his so-called business parties or when they would venture out in public together. Just like the one she heard he was throwing in two days. He didn't know that she knew about it. Since her leg injury, she had managed to avoid attending the scaled down get-togethers, though she had helped in planning them. To Mitchell's credit, he had kept them low-key, and they turned out to be more of a poker night with the guys. But the event he was planning for Sunday looked like he was getting back into the swing of things. That made her very nervous.

Not only was she the one who cooked all the food and did all the prep work, but she was also expected to play hostess and entertain the guests. They mainly consisted of Mitchell's buddies, who tended to get a little handsy after they'd been drinking. What pissed her off even more was that Mitchell allowed it to happen even after she voiced her displeasure.

She took a seat on the bed. It was time to start putting her plans in place to get out of town. She needed to make sure she had a perfect, well-executed plan so he wouldn't be able to track her down like he had the last two times. She swore he had installed a LoJack system on her.

She never publicly admitted to anyone that Mitchell was behind her bruises and other so-called accidents. She knew people talked and wondered why she stayed with him, but they didn't understand his control over her.

At the time of her father's accident, she was in such a grieving state that she didn't think twice when Mitchell came to her and offered her a place to stay. Where else was she going to go? The only money she had was from working a few shifts at the diner, which covered her gas and groceries. She just hadn't realized the monster Mitchell was. After her mom died, Campbell had put all her focus on dancing. Her dad made sure of that.

She grabbed some clothes out of her dresser and made her way to the bathroom. She started the shower and began to remove her clothes when she heard him.

"Belle?"

She cringed, hearing his pet name for her. He told her that she didn't seem like a "Campbell," so he called her Belle.

She thought about ignoring him but quickly changed her mind. She wasn't in the mood for confrontation. Things had been rocky between them since he had shown the worst side of him and nearly caused her to have her leg amputated. To his credit, he had stuck to their agreement and had given her space, but she could tell over the last few weeks that his patience was wearing. She could see the hunger in his eyes.

She turned the water off and limped back into the bedroom. She was shocked when she found him going through her purse. It wasn't like she had anything to hide, plus she knew better than to try and keep something around the house that she didn't want to be found. Unbeknownst to him, she had rented a storage locker two towns over and had slowly moved the majority of her personal belongings there. That was so when she finally did find a way out of his house of horrors, she wouldn't have to worry about leaving anything vital behind. She kept boxes around the guest house to make it look like she had her things there, but they were just filled with junk.

"What are you doing?" She asked him.

Totally ignoring her question, he gave her that sleazy smile of his, and she wondered if he had been drinking.

"I wanted to see how your day was."

He stepped toward her and tried to kiss her, but she turned her head, making his lips press against her cheek. She tried to step to the side, but he grabbed her arm, and she froze.

"Don't!" He barked at her, and she snapped her eyes to his, hearing the warning in his tone.

"Don't shy away from me. Enough is enough. I've given you what you asked for. I've proven myself to you. You belong back under my roof with me. We belong together."

"You told me when I was ready," she countered and wanted to pull the words back when he glared at her.

He looked around at all the boxes, and she prayed he wouldn't open any of them since they were meant as show.

He released her. "I'm hosting a few friends tonight and I need you to whip up something." He ran his finger down her cheek. "Please say you'll help me. You know I can't do it without you."

That was the last thing she wanted to do. She pulled away, putting some distance between them. "I don't think that's a good idea, plus I thought you weren't hosting anyone until Sunday." She knew his buddies and how they could get.

If she wasn't dancing, she loved dreaming up themed events. Before her dad's untimely death and when she and he used to hang out with some of his coworkers, she would help plan some of his friends' kids' birthday parties and other festive engagements.

Mitchell closed the space between them, causing her to take another step backward, but she ended up with the wall against her back. He glided his fingers down her arm, causing a shiver to wrack her body. As much as she wanted to pull away, she knew better.

"I'm exhausted tonight. Why don't you and your friends order something to be delivered?"

He took a strand of her strawberry blonde hair and twirled it around his finger as he stared deep into her eyes. She knew just from his look that her time of freedom had come to an end.

He pressed his body firmly against her, trapping her against the wall. He wedged his thick thigh between her legs. She pushed him off, but he grabbed her wrists and restrained them behind her back. He squeezed them tighter, and she knew she'd be bruised. He gripped her hair and neck with his other hand.

She lost her breath as her eyes locked on his. They were dark and cold. The evilness poured from them. She knew she was up to her ass in alligators.

He lowered his head and pressed his mouth against her neck. She closed her eyes as he licked her skin before moving to her chin and nipping it.

"Be a good girl, Belle, and obey me. If you don't cooperate, I'll let Kent do as he pleases with you when he gets here." He ran his hand down her arm that was immobile from him restraining her. "And trust me, sweetheart, I don't want to see your face messed up." He smiled down at her. "After all, it's your number one feature. Well, besides that pussy of yours. But that is for my pleasure only." He licked his lips. "It's been too long."

She was disgusted. He hadn't changed at all, but now she was at his mercy. He was too strong for her.

He pulled her away from the wall and pushed her onto the bed. At first, she stilled, fearing what he was going to do to her. But then she remembered what she promised herself in the hospital—she wasn't going to be the victim anymore. God, she only needed another week or two, and she would've been home free.

He pulled his shirt off before removing his belt. She couldn't, in her good conscience, just lie there and let him manipulate her however he wanted.

He started to cover her body with his, and she swung her head forward and headbutted him. He shouted and covered his nose with his hands. She rolled to the side and made a run for the door. Her damn limp cost her precious time as Mitchell caught up to her and pulled her back by her hair. She cried out. It felt as if he had yanked a handful of her hair out.

He swung her around and backhanded her across the face. She fell to the floor in between a chair and the dresser. When she looked up, she honestly thought she was staring at Satan. He had blood dripping out of his nose, but it was the killer look he gave her.

"Wrong move, sweetheart." He told her as he lifted his arm into the air. That was when she realized he was going to hit her with his belt. She covered her head just as the slap of the belt was felt across her forearms.

Whack! Whack!

Goddammit! She bit her lip so hard to keep from screaming out in pain that she tasted blood. He didn't let up. His lashes only became more violent. Her arms felt raw, and they stung.

When no more strikes to her body came, only then did she attempt to look at him. Her vision was blurry from all the tears. When she made eye contact with him, he looked delusional. He stared at her arms and the damage he had done to them. She saw the blood oozing from some of the wounds. The skin along both of her arms was so red that it even felt hot to touch.

He reached for her, and she flinched, fearing what his next move would be. He grabbed her chin and made her look at him.

"Look what you made me do!" He screamed at her as she continued to cry.

He dropped his hand and stood over her as she sought shelter in the small space she was in.

"Clean yourself up. You have two days to get your shit moved back into the main house. I'm leaving for a business trip tomorrow morning. When I return in a few days, it better be your face that I see when I first walk through the front doors. And for your sake, I hope you listen."

Without another word, he grabbed his shirt off the bed and left.

As soon as she heard the front door slam, she lost it. She was so distraught that she couldn't stop her body from shaking. She looked down at her arms. They looked awful. She managed to get herself up and into the bathroom.

She stared at her reflection in the mirror. She had red marks all over her body where the belt missed her arms. But the open wounds on her arms concerned her, and her skin was already starting to bruise.

"I will not be a victim any longer," she said to herself and vowed that she would find a way out before Mitchell's deadline.

CHAPTER FIVE

Fred carried the tray of four coffees over to the table of the four men that Derek sent.

Belle was due to arrive in about fifteen minutes for her shift, though he was concerned that she might not show. She had called in sick her last two shifts, and he was beginning to worry about her, especially when she hadn't responded to him when he asked if she was okay.

She hadn't been initially scheduled for today's shift. But to get her here when the guys arrived, he made up a story about the county health inspector coming for the diner's annual inspection and that he needed her help to get the back storage area ready. He also knew she was looking for extra hours, so he didn't think she'd bat an eye. But something in her voice, the slight hesitation in her response, made him think she may try to make an excuse not to come. Belle assured him through a text that she'd be there.

He set the tray down on the table, and the guys all took their drinks. He pulled a chair up to the table.

"I can't tell you guys how much I appreciate you coming up here, especially on such short notice."

"Not a problem. Derek explained a little. Well, at least what you had told him. We're glad we could help."

Fred looked at Diego. "Diego, Derek said you're in the process of remodeling your home."

Diego nodded but appeared annoyed. "I am. But unfortunately, I'm sidelined from that too."

Fred felt for the guy. He'd gone through a similar situation, but in Fred's case, his injury had been a career-ending one. Taking a bullet in the lung was all that it took.

"It's all good, though. I wouldn't have said yes if I didn't mean it. As I told Derek, I've got more than enough room. She'll have her own private space."

"Can you give us a little background on her situation?" Ace asked.

"She's an amazing woman. She's somewhat shy, but if you push her enough, there is a lioness within her." Fred smiled.

Potter chuckled. "Sounds like some other women we know very well." And the others all nodded their heads in agreement, knowing that Potter was referencing Alex, Tenley, Autumn, Bailey, Mia, Arianna, and now Anna Grace being added to that mix.

"How did she end up with this guy to begin with?" Diego asked.

"Belle and her dad moved to the area about five or six years ago after her mom died. Her dad worked for the guy's mining company. About two years ago, her dad was killed in an explosion underground."

"Jesus. That's terrible," Irish said.

Fred grimaced. "Yeah, it was. Investigators said that the explosion was due to a gas leak. Anyway, poor Belle had been in a total state of shock and despair. Mitchell, the guy in question, swooped in like some fucking hero. He was well aware that she didn't have anything since her dad was footing all the bills and rent while she finished college and concentrated on her dancing career."

"She's a dancer?" Diego asked, setting his cup down on the table.

"Used to be," Fred snarled. "Until about a year ago when she had an unfortunate accident."

"What aren't you saying?" Diego asked.

"I don't want to speculate, but that no good son of a bitch has hurt her more than once. He's controlling and knows he has her pinned against a wall. It doesn't help when he has the judges, the city council, and attorneys all in his back pocket."

"Law enforcement?" Ace questioned.

"They hate him, but their hands are tied because of the city. Mitchell Langford pretty much controls this entire town."

Something across the street caught Fred's eye. He looked and focused on the person emerging from the wooded area. They wore a black hooded sweatshirt with the hood pulled up so he couldn't see the face, but he realized who it was as soon as he noticed the slight limp.

"What the hell?" He muttered and stood from the chair. Something was wrong. Where was her truck?

"Shit! That's her." He said to the table and quickly rushed to the door to unlock it.

Diego was curious to meet the woman who was going to be staying with him. Listening to the little bit that Fred explained, it sounded like she'd been dealt a shitty hand at life.

As Fred hurried to meet the woman, Belle, Diego's eyes were fixed on her as she walked across the parking lot. Immediately he became concerned because she was limping. She looked petite even with the bulky hoodie she was wearing. She had the hood pulled up and her head down so he couldn't see her face. As she approached the door, Fred appeared frantic as he flipped the lock and opened the door for her. He couldn't hear their exchange, but when she threw herself into Fred's arms, Diego realized then just how special the woman was to Fred and his wife. He would make damn sure she was protected under his roof.

Once Fred got her inside, he relocked the door since the place wasn't due to open for another forty-five minutes. When the woman lowered her hood, and her face came into view, Diego was overcome with anger. In fact, everyone at the table saw the bruising along her cheek. It was evident from her reaction to Fred and the bruise that she had been involved in an altercation of some sort.

Stella, Fred's wife, rushed out from the back looking concerned and began fussing over the woman. Right before Stella ushered the woman back toward the kitchen, Fred said something to her, and she briefly glanced over toward their table.

Fred glanced over at the table and held his finger up, signaling to them to give him a minute before he followed Stella and the woman to the back.

"I have a feeling that's our girl," Ace said, appearing upset.

"Did you see her face?" Irish asked, and all of them nodded.

"She looked terrified. You can see it in her body language," Potter said, taking a sip of his coffee as he kept his eye on the kitchen door.

Diego picked up his cup of coffee and took a sip as his mind began to venture into places that had him pissed off. Someone had hurt her, and that wasn't acceptable.

Fred walked through the doors of the kitchen and found Stella and Belle in a tight hug. Both of them had tears in their eyes.

"Belle, what's going on? How did you get that bruise on your cheek?" She went to speak, but he held his hand up and gave her a stern fatherly warning. "I don't want to hear another excuse come from your mouth. I want the truth." He stood there with his fists clenched by his sides. He knew exactly how she acquired it. But he wanted to hear it from her directly.

A tear slipped out of her eye, and she quickly wiped it away.

"I'm not going back to Mitchell's after I finish my shift today."

More tears started to fall, and Fred took her elbow and guided her out of the way of George, the cook. He was concerned and also interested in what caused this sudden decision of hers.

"What do you mean you're leaving? Where are you going?"

She shrugged her shoulders. "I don't know yet. I just know that I'm done. I can't take it anymore." She lowered her eyes. "I haven't been honest with you guys, and believe me, it killed me to stay silent. But I knew there was nothing that you or anyone else could do because Mitchell has his claws everything and everyone." She started to pace the length of the kitchen, and Fred let her, knowing it was her way of gathering and getting her thoughts out. "I had a lot of time to think while I was laid up in the hospital, no thanks to Mitchell. The day I was released into his care was the day I started plotting my plan to get the hell out of here. I may not know where I'm headed, but as long as he can't find me, that's all I care about."

Fred sat there and listened to her explain what she'd been up to for the last few months. And he had to admit that he was pretty impressed, though he was peeved that she hadn't come to him for help. One thing he was very interested in that he would talk to her about later was the evidence she had submitted to the Division of Mining and Reclamation proving that Mitchell was operating the mine at dangerous levels, not to mention illegally tampering with the machinery log-books.

"Belle, you can't do this all on your own, honey. You need help."

She shook her head in defiance. "No. I'm not going to involve you or Stella. You both have done so much for me already. I don't want to see either of you get put in the middle and then have Mitchell targeting you."

"It's a little late for that. Stella and I care very much about you. And to let you in on a secret, you aren't the only one who's been planning a way to get you out of here."

Her eyes widened. "What?"

He smirked. "Do me a favor and deliver that tray of food to the table of gentlemen while I speak with Stella. Then we'll talk about how you're getting out of this town. But it's going to be my way, and with a little bit of backup."

Surprisingly, Belle nodded, though she still appeared shocked. She stood and pulled her hoodie off. She was wearing another long-sleeved t-shirt.

Once she was out of earshot, Fred looked at Stella and grinned. "At least we know she's not going to put up a fight about leaving."

"I'm worried about her. Do you think she'll be okay?" Stella asked and appeared upset. Fred pulled her into a hug.

"Don't worry, sweetheart. Belle is going to be just fine. From what Derek said, she's going to be in good hands."

Stella looked up at him and grinned. "That Diego fella is handsome."

Fred rolled his eyes and groaned. "Oh, dear lord. You always have to play the matchmaker."

She playfully slapped his chest. "Oh, hush. I'd love to see Belle find love in the arms of a good man. Just like I found you."

He smiled and placed a kiss on her temple.

Campbell lifted the tray of food and felt the ache in her lower arms. Mitchell had done a hell of a job on her with the belt. In another world, she'd love to have the opportunity to repay the favor. When she cleaned and wrapped them in gauze before leaving the house, they were red, swollen, and some marks still seeped fluid. Breathing through the bite of pain, she balanced the tray on her shoulder and headed towards the table. She wondered who the men were, considering the diner wasn't even open for business yet.

As she approached the booth where the four huge men were sitting, she felt her heart start to race as all four sets of eyes turned in her direction. And they didn't appear happy. She hoped it wasn't because their food order took so long. She flashed the smile she was trained to show.

"Hi. Sorry for the delay." She lifted the plate with the scrambled eggs, toast, sausage links, and hashbrowns. "Who gets the number four?"

The biggest guy of the four gave her a soft smile. "That's me, honey."

She smiled and handed him the plate. She then handed over the two pancake breakfasts to the two men sitting on the end. She looked at the fourth guy sitting on the inside, against the window.

"I guess you're number one." She stated as she passed him the plate of two eggs over easy, bacon, English muffin, and home fries. *Damn, these guys could eat.*

The guy took the plate and smiled. "Thanks."

The blonde hair and blue-eyed guy sitting next to him smirked. "Now you've just inflated his ego by calling him number one."

She knew he meant it as a joke, but she felt her cheeks redden, realizing what that may have sounded like. Wanting to make a quick exit, she noticed they were all low on coffee.

"I'll be right back with some more coffee. Anything else I can get you?"

The guy sitting on the end with jet black hair and piercing blue eyes smiled. "I think we're good. But more coffee would be great. Thank you."

As the guys began to dig into their food, she walked behind the counter and made a fresh pot of coffee. As the coffee brewed, she kept taking small glances towards the table, and every so often, she'd catch the guy who ordered the number one looking at her. She snorted a laugh. All four were handsome, but the guy with the olive complexion, shaved head, and five o'clock shadow was really the number one in her book. She shook her head in disbelief. Fantasizing about men was the last thing she should be doing.

She heard the coffee maker sputter, signaling that it was finished. She grabbed the fresh pot of coffee and walked back over to the table.

"Here you are, some fresh hot coffee." She said, ignoring their glances as she topped off each cup, and they each said thank you and offered her a friendly smile.

Just as she was about to leave the table, Fred walked up behind her and rested his hands on her shoulders. She tilted her head back and grinned up at him.

"How's the chow?" He asked the guys.

The guy on the end who seemed to take charge answered. "Everything's delicious. Now we know why Derek said to leave enough time to eat."

Fred laughed and squeezed Campbell's shoulders before he pulled up a second chair and told her to have a seat.

She gave him a questionable look, wondering what was going on. Stella then approached and took the coffee pot from her and told her that everything would be fine and to sit and listen to what Fred had to say.

Fred pulled up another chair beside her and took a seat.

"Belle, I would like to introduce you to Ace, Potter, Irish, and Diego."

She met the eyes of each man. "It's nice to meet you," she said, and she damned her nerves upon hearing the shakiness in her voice.

Ace, the guy sitting on the end, again, flashed her a big smile. "It's nice to meet you as well, Belle."

Fred then took over the conversation. "Belle, remember back in the kitchen when I told you that I've been working on a plan to help get you out of here?"

She didn't speak but nodded her head.

"Well, I called a very good friend of mine. He and I served together. And we came up with a game plan that I believe will give you what you're looking for—freedom to live your life the way you want to."

She stared at him. "How?"

He grinned then nodded toward the gentlemen sitting at the table. "Them. They work with Derek, my friend, and they came here as a favor to help you."

She looked at them and swallowed hard. "Why would you do that?" She found herself asking them.

"Where we come from, we're taught to assist those in need. We understand how this probably comes as a shock to you, but believe us when we say we would like nothing more than to help you out of the mess you're in. And as Fred said, you'll have your life back."

She pulled her bottom lip in between her teeth as she looked from Fred and back to the guys. Could this really be happening? Could these guys really help her?

"So, you want me to go with these men? What happens then? Where would I live?" She fired off questions rapidly as her mind was on overdrive.

Before Fred could answer her, Diego, her number one, spoke.

"Belle, we are honest-to-god men. We have a robust system back home in Virginia Beach. Some of us have wives and children, not to mention we have many friends who have our back. If you decide to come with us, they will have your back as well.

As for your question about where you'll stay, you'll be staying at my place. I have more than enough room."

Ace then followed up on Diego's comments. "What we're offering you—is a chance at a clean slate, and it probably isn't going to come along again, especially with the protection we're offering to go along with it."

"How will it work? I mean, will I be under your command? Will I have to obey everything you say? Because if so, I don't think I can handle that. Those are the actions that I'm trying to get away from."

"Sweetheart, nobody is going to control you. Nor do we want to." Diego assured her.

She wasn't sure why her eyes began to fill with tears considering this was the strangest thing, but they were right. When would another opportunity like this come along?

Just as she was ready to tell them that she'd do it, Stella's frantic voice shouting from behind the counter had her diving for cover.

"Oh, God. Vinny and his crew just pulled up."

Campbell felt all the blood drain from her face. They must've already found the car she parked on the other side of town—damn tracking devices.

She met Diego's eyes and quickly apologized before dropping to her knees and crawling under the table. In her hasty retreat, she clipped the edge of the table with her forehead. She grunted in pain but continued. There wasn't a whole lot of room for her with four sets of long legs stretched out. She needed to get as close as she could to the wall to avoid being seen if they walked near the table. She started to climb over Diego's jean-covered legs, but he moved his one leg, letting her through. She waited for him to move his other leg so she could sit against the wall, but he never moved it. Instead, he reached under the table and pulled her in-between his large thick thighs where her back was against the bottom of the booth. Once she was settled, he positioned his legs to form a barrier around her. If she weren't so afraid of Vinny finding her, she'd be laughing up a storm, knowing how ridiculous she probably looked. She took a glance at their feet. All four of them wore a type of hiking boot, and they were huge. They had to be size eleven and up. They were giant men, and she knew already that if she got out of the current situation without Vinny finding her, she would go with these men, no questions asked. She trusted Fred. And if Fred said they were good people, then she'd accept their offer.

Diego felt Campbell settle in the space between his legs. Potter, who was sitting across from him, smirked. All four men looked at one another, and Ace gave them a quick hand signal for them to play this out. They all started to dig into their meals as if a frightened woman wasn't hiding under their table.

Three men stood at the front door, and one man pounded on the glass so hard that Diego thought he might bust it. Fred appeared calm and walked to unlock it. Diego had caught a glimpse of the trio as they emerged from the black Ford Expedition. He saw the gun on the one guy's hip and was pretty confident that the other two were carrying as well.

"What can I do for you, Vinny?" Fred questioned the first guy as he opened the door.

"We're looking for Belle. She said she was working at the diner today, but we just found her car down at the gas station by the interchange."

Vinny then noticed the four of them sitting in the booth.

"Who are they?" Diego heard him ask Fred.

"Friends of mine," Fred replied, then diverted the conversation away from the team. "Belle wasn't scheduled to work today. She's not here."

The Vinny guy ran his hand through his hair. He appeared nervous, and Diego wondered why.

Just then, Stella walked up and stood next to Fred.

"What's going on? Did you say Belle was missing?" She asked the guy, playing along and appearing genuinely concerned.

"Well, Stella, it seems Belle has disappeared again," Vinny said, then gave both Fred and Stella a scrutinized look. "You don't happen to know her whereabouts, would you? And before you try and cover for her, remember that Mitchell doesn't tolerate being lied to by anyone."

Diego knew that the guys were ready to interfere at any second. But at the moment, he was more concerned about the fearful woman sitting under the table and taking shelter between his legs. Her right shoulder was touching his knee, and when Vinny would speak, she'd start to tremble.

Diego watched as Stella squared her shoulders and narrowed her eyes. "Are you threatening me?"

"All I'm saying is if you are trying to cover for the little bitch, then you better watch your back when Mitchell returns."

Diego heard Belle's faint gasp when Vinny issued the threat against Fred and Stella. He reached under the table with one hand while he used the other to eat some eggs even though the food was the last thing on his mind. When his hand landed on her shoulder, she tried to move away, but he squeezed the delicate shoulder and tightened his legs around her body. He was afraid that if she tried to move, she would draw attention to them. When she seemed to get his message, he tapped her shoulder again, letting her know she was safe. She must have understood because she covered his hand with hers and squeezed it back. He was shocked how her gentle touch did a number to his insides, especially when he felt her relax back in-between his legs. He wondered where this instant possessiveness was coming from, but he didn't want to let her go. Something told him that he wanted to learn everything there was about her. But first, they had to get rid of the three douchebags.

He watched out of his peripheral vision as Vinny and another man questioned Fred and Stella about Belle. The third guy thought he was slick and slipped behind the counter and into the kitchen, probably looking to see if Belle was back there hiding. He and the guys started to make small talk about their trip back home, but he knew damn well each of them was listening to every word Vinny was saying.

"Do you remember what happened to Belle when Mitchell found her the last time she tried to run?"

"What makes you think she's running? Did you ever think she could be at the shopping center just across the street from the gas station? Many people park across the street and walk over because it's easier to get in and out. And if I'm correct, wasn't she there one other time that Mitchell thought she ran off? Although I couldn't blame her if she tried."

Vinny pointed at Stella and gave her a mean look. "You best watch what you say, lady. For Belle's sake, I hope she's at the store. Because if she isn't, Mitchell is going to be pissed that he'll have to cut short his business trip to come home and deal with her recalcitrant behavior. And, you know as well as I do, it won't bode well for her.

Fred crossed his arms and stared at Vinny. "No. I don't know. Would you like to enlighten me? Belle doesn't talk about her home life. But I'm no fool. I know she isn't happy, and I hope to hell she escapes the violence."

Diego could hear the anger coming off Fred just in his voice alone. He was beginning to worry that the conversation could turn violent. They needed to get these assholes out of the diner so they could plan an exit strategy because if he were those assholes, he'd have someone watching the place. So, getting Campbell out without being seen could be a challenge.

"I guess you'll have to go look for her, Vinny. After all, I thought it was your job to look after her? As we've said, we haven't seen her or heard from her since her shift three days ago."

Vinny rubbed his jaw as if he was thinking. Finally, he gave the nod to the other two men with him, and together they all exited the diner and piled into a vehicle. As they were walking to the car, Diego didn't miss Vinny glance their way through the window. He memorized each of their faces in case they showed up in Virginia Beach.

As Campbell sat hiding from the monsters that came looking for her, she felt the tears build in her eyes. Listening to the banter had her thinking about how stupid she was to keep going back to Mitchell. Every time she had tried to escape, it only got worse. She knew that eventually the punishment would be death. It was just a matter of time.

Her body trembled, and she felt the hand on her shoulder. It was large, and she felt the warmth emanate from his touch. She should be afraid of a man's touch. Hands like Mitchell's only hurt and abused women. But number one's hand was gentle and soothing.

When she heard Vinny threaten Stella, she almost gave herself away when she went to crawl out from under the table, but the hand on her shoulder squeezed, and his legs wrapped around her holding her in place. When she stilled, his hand caressed, then lightly tapped her shoulder. She couldn't move, nor did she want to move. His comfort was infectious, and she found herself leaning into him.

When Campbell heard the bell on the diner's door chime, she sagged with relief. She couldn't believe she actually crawled under a table full of customers. And not just any customers—four huge ass men that looked like they could chew up Vinny and spit him out.

She felt a little embarrassed. *Frickity, fudge sticks.* How was she going to face these guys after what they just heard?

When she crawled out from under the table, Stella was already making her way over to her. She had tears in her eyes, and Campbell felt guilty for putting Fred and Stella through that ordeal. She felt her own tears start to burn her eyes.

Stella wrapped her up in a hug, and Campbell hugged her back. She knew that Vinny's departure was only temporary. He'd keep coming back until he was satisfied that she wasn't at the diner. She needed to get far away from this town and its people. Well, except for Patty and Fred.

"Oh child, I thought for sure Vinny saw you through the window when he pulled in."

"I'm so sorry, Stella. All I've done is bring trouble to your door." She then turned and faced the four men and wiped the tears from her face the best she could, but they kept falling. She specifically sought out Diego, her number one. "Now that you've seen firsthand what I'm up against, are you sure you're up for this? If you're not, I'll understand completely."

Diego could sense her hesitation, and he understood. They were total strangers to her. She didn't know anything about them, but he needed to convince her that going with him was her best option.

He nudged Irish in the shoulder and motioned for him to slide out of the booth so he could get up.

Once he was on his feet and standing next to her, he slowly and gently took her tiny hand in his. He was relieved she didn't try to pull away. She looked up at him, and that was when he got a really good look at her eyes. They were hazel, with specks of gold that complimented her hair color.

She was beautiful. She was tiny compared to his six-foot frame. She reminded him of a little pixie with her button nose.

"Belle, one thing you need to know about us is that if we don't want to do something, we won't. But we're here because we want to be here. I know you're probably hesitant and have concerns. After all, you don't know us. But you have our word—my word, in front of both Fred and Stella that we'll protect you. That doesn't mean we'll try and control you, though; we may offer you some advice now and then. But starting now, you belong to nobody but yourself."

He could feel her tiny body shaking, and he wanted to pull her in for a big hug and reiterate to her that he would protect her. Instead, he tucked a strand of hair behind her ear and smiled.

She took a deep breath. "I don't have anything but the clothes on my back and two outfits in my backpack. I have some money saved that I can give you for rent."

"With one phone call, you'll have a closet full of clothes by the time you arrive in Virginia Beach." Ace told her, and Diego didn't doubt that. Alex and the others would hook her up.

"As far as paying rent—that's not happening. Consider yourself a guest. As I told Fred, I have more than enough room for you."

She looked at Fred and Stella, and Diego saw the tears glistening in her eyes. He didn't want her to cry. "Fred, are you sure?" She asked.

Fred walked over and embraced her. "Belle, I trust these men with my life. What they're offering is freedom. This is your chance to take your life back and live it how you want to. Take the opportunity and run with it."

She sniffled. "I'm going to miss you and Stella."

"We'll miss you too, but don't worry, we'll find a way to communicate with each other. Right now, we just need you to get to a safe place."

She turned towards the guys. Her eyes sought out Diego again, and that small gesture made his chest tighten just a little.

"Can you guys give me five minutes to clean myself up?"

"How about we give you ten, doll," Irish said, winking at her trying to lighten up the mood a little.

CHAPTER SIX

Campbell sat sandwiched between Diego and Irish in the back seat of the truck. They had been on the road for about an hour, and for the most part, it had been a quiet ride. Occasionally, one of the guys would say something, but that was about the extent of any conversation.

Fred had mentioned that these guys work for their commander, so she assumed they were military. She wondered what they did. Since nobody else filled the awkward silence, she decided she would.

"You guys are in the military, right?" When she didn't get an immediate response, she continued. "At least that's what Fred told me. He didn't say exactly what you do, but I would assume you work on a ship and travel the world."

She thought she heard Potter snort a small laugh from the front passenger seat.

"We do a little more than that," Diego told her, and she looked up at him.

"What does that mean? What *do* you do?" She pressed, and she noticed that Diego met Ace's eyes in the rearview mirror.

When Diego looked back at her, he licked his lower lip.

"Do you know what SEALs are?"

She gave him an odd look at first, but then her expression softened, and she smiled. *Let's see if I can lighten up the mood in here.*

"Of course, I know what seals are," she told him, her tone insinuating that he asked a dumb question. "They're the cutest little animals with their little whiskers and flippers. I don't know which is my favorite; the brown ones or the gray ones with black spots. It's so hard to choose. Do you have a favorite?" She asked the group.

When she saw Diego's eyes widen, followed by Irish's and Potter's heads twisting to look at her as if she had completely lost her mind, she couldn't hold in the laughter any longer.

She started cracking up laughing while holding her stomach. Diego went to say something, but she held her hand up. "I'm just messing with you guys. Of course, I know what SEALs are. Fred was one. And isn't the correct name for a SEAL a Special Warfare Operator?"

She grinned when she heard Potter and Ace chuckle. Irish looked at Diego with a huge smile on his face.

"She's going to fit in perfectly with the others." He told Diego, and she wondered who Irish was talking about. But Diego just continued staring at her. After a few seconds, he finally cracked a small smile.

"Aren't you just a little smart-ass?" He said jokingly, and it made her laugh again.

"Sorry, I just had to. You guys looked so serious."

Speaking to the group, she said, "I respect what you guys do, although I don't know exactly what you do. I mean, the news talks about stuff, but even I know that's only half the truth if even that." God, she was rambling. "I guess what I'm trying to say is thank you for serving and protecting those of us here at home."

Diego looked down at her. "Thank you, and you're welcome."

They talked for a bit longer, telling her things about Virginia Beach until she fought to keep her eyes open. She felt both physically and mentally drained. Now that the shock of everything had worn off, she felt that if she closed her eyes, she might not wake up for a few days. Without the immediate threat of Mitchell or Vinny breathing down her neck, she felt like she could relax for a bit. However, it would be a difficult transition after looking over her shoulder for the last few years.

Before the night that Mitchell put her in the hospital when she lived with him, he didn't allow her much sleep. He considered sleeping a waste of time and expected her to stay up with him, and some nights even entertain him. He also expected her to keep the house clean. And she never wanted to do anything that made him angry, because an unhappy Mitchell meant punishment for her.

She cringed, thinking of the ways he used to punish her. If she messed up a meal, he wouldn't allow her to eat for twenty-four hours. If his cigar ashtrays weren't cleaned right away, he would burn her the next time he smoked one. Thank goodness that had only happened twice. She had the scars on her inner thighs as a reminder.

"Have you ever been to Virginia Beach, Belle?" Potter asked from the front seat, bringing her mind back to the present.

"No." She wasn't about to tell them she had only been out of West Virginia twice. Once for a recital in Pittsburgh, and once for her audition in Cleveland. They would really think she was lame.

"Belle?" She looked up at Diego, and he was looking at her. *Dang, had he asked me something?*

"I'm sorry, what did you ask?"

"I asked if you would like to take a nap. We still have a couple of hours."

Instead of answering him, she said, "Campbell." Since these men were doing her a favor, she only thought it was right to tell them her real name. Plus, she actually liked her name even though Mitchell didn't.

Diego tilted his head. "What?"

"My name is Campbell."

"I thought it was Belle. That's what Fred called you."

"Mitchell didn't like Campbell, so he called me Belle. I didn't want to argue with him, so I just accepted the name and went by it."

She could tell that Diego wasn't pleased with that information.

"What would *you* like to go by? Remember, this is your life, sweetheart. And just for the record, Campbell is a beautiful name."

She stared deep into his dark chocolate eyes. Was this guy for real? Were all the men in her company right now always this sincere?

"I'd like to go by my given name, if that's okay."

He gave her a killer smile that made her belly do a flip. "Of course, it is. Now, if you're tired, lean on me and try to get some sleep."

Campbell said goodbye to Ace, Potter, and Irish before following Diego up to the front door of the large home. She was in awe of his property. The house was a two-story single-family home with an attached three-car garage. Diego unlocked the front door and motioned for her to go in. As she stepped into the foyer, Diego followed and disarmed the alarm. She looked around at the spacious open floor plan. Diego hadn't been lying when he said he had more than enough room. She did notice that he didn't have much furniture.

He set his bag down and placed his keys on a table next to the door.

"Welcome home." He told her and guided her further inside.

"This is beautiful. Have you been doing all the work yourself?"

"Mostly. The guys help now and then when it's a larger project, and I need a hand."

She smiled. "It must be nice to take something down to the bones and make it yours." She walked into the kitchen and almost had heart palpitations. It was stunning. She ran her hand across the smooth white and grey granite. She looked up and saw the wooden beams built into the ceiling.

She pointed up at the beams. "Did you remove the walls?"

"I did." He looked her over. "You seem to know a bit about construction yourself."

She shrugged her shoulders. "Some. I learned most of it from watching and helping my dad around our place."

Changing the subject, she asked. "What else do you have left?"

He blew out a big breath. "Believe it or not, quite a bit. Though most of the major remodeling is complete, there are still many items to get through. But I don't know when I'll be able to do any of it. Not until my doctors say I can do anything strenuous."

She eyed him over. "If you don't mind me asking, how did it occur?"

"How did what occur?"

"Your head injury."

He squinted his eyes. "How did you know it was a head injury?" He questioned her and seemed to be on the defensive, and she feared she may have stepped over the line.

"I—I noticed you rubbing it a lot. Is there anything I get you, or do for you?" She felt awkward but thought it was the right thing to ask.

"I'm fine." He stated his words with a little bit of a bite, which immediately put her on guard. She started to back away, and he stepped forward.

"Campbell—"

"It's fine. I'm sorry for pushing. Plus, it's none of my business. Do you mind showing me where I'll be sleeping?"

That was not how she wanted to start their time together. As they approached the stairs, she touched his arm but dropped her hand quickly when he looked down at her.

"I just wanted to say thank you again."

He didn't say anything but nodded before he started up the curved staircase, and she followed him. Once they made it to the top, Diego directed her to the right. He showed her three bedrooms which were empty and still needed some work. As they approached the end of the hall, there was another door. He opened it and flipped the light on.

"This'll be your room," he told her and motioned for her to enter.

She walked in and set her backpack down. The walls in the room were painted a soft grey color. The bold cherry red accents placed moderately throughout the room captured her attention and gave the room some pizazz.

"Will it do?" Diego asked from behind her as he leaned against the doorway, watching her.

Would it do? She thought to herself.

"Diego, this is beautiful."

"It's yours for however long you want it."

She stood in the middle of the room, looking at him. He pushed off the doorway and took a step closer.

"Listen, Campbell. I'm sorry for getting a little short earlier downstairs."

Now she felt awful. He had nothing to be sorry for. She shouldn't have stuck her nose into something she shouldn't have.

"I think I should be the one to apologize. I had no business questioning you."

He shifted on his feet as if he was nervous, and she wondered why. Then he changed the subject as he nodded toward a few shopping bags sitting near the closet door.

"Those are for you. Alex, Ace's fiancée, picked up a few things for you."

She walked over and peeked inside the bags. They were stuffed full of clothing, and one was nothing but toiletries. Once she was alone, she would go through it. She turned back toward Diego.

"That was very nice of her. If I don't get a chance to meet her, please tell her that I said thank you."

He nodded his head. "Well, I'll let you get settled. If you need anything, my room is at the opposite end of the hall."

As he turned to walk out, she called his name. "Diego."

He looked over his shoulder. "Yeah."

"Thank you."

"You're welcome, Campbell."

He closed the door behind him. Campbell walked over to the bed and sat down. It was a very comfortable mattress. She laid back and closed her eyes. God, she hoped she made the right choice. As she laid there thinking of all the events leading up to this moment, she started to drift off, and before she knew it, she was fast asleep.

Diego felt like shit as he walked from Campbell's room and down the stairs. He hadn't meant to snap at her. She was just asking a simple question. Hell, he probably would've asked a similar question if he were in her shoes.

He wondered how she sustained that limp she walked with. It was the one thing that Fred hadn't mentioned. Well, he had plenty of time to find out. He just hoped he hadn't caused a setback between the two of them.

He went to the kitchen to get a bottle of water from the refrigerator and some acetaminophen to ease the pain he was feeling in his head. He returned to the living room and took a seat in his recliner. He popped the pills into his mouth and washed them down with a slug of water.

He grabbed his phone off the table and dialed Alex.

"Hey, Diego," Alex answered, and Diego grinned.

"Hi, Alex."

"How's your house guest?"

"She's doing okay. I think."

"You think?"

He ran his hand over his head. "I think I might have upset her."

"Sheesh. She's only been there for what, forty-five minutes or so? What happened?"

"It was all me and my insecurity. She called out my injury, and I sort of snapped at her, and I think I hurt her feelings. I feel like shit about it."

"Did you apologize?"

"Of course, but she kind of clammed up and is up in her room."

"I'm sure it'll be fine."

"I hope so. Anyway, I just wanted to call and say thank you. I saw all the bags you left in the room for her. Just let me know what I owe you."

"Oh. You're welcome. And don't worry about paying me back. You know I'd do anything for you guys."

Diego loved Alex like a sister. She was one of the most giving people he knew. She was also one of the bravest women he knew. Not many men or women could've survived the physical abuse she endured when she was kidnapped in Afghanistan, let alone kill five of her captors before she was rescued. She was an amazing woman and one he was proud to call a friend.

"So, when do I get to meet her?" Alex asked, and Diego grinned. He was positive that Alex and the rest of the ladies of Alpha Team were jumping at the bit to get an introduction to Campbell.

"I don't know if I'll let you." He teased.

"Hey. That's not fair. Ace said she seems really sweet, and she's pretty."

Diego rolled his eyes. He knew where this conversation was heading, and he needed to cut it off. Alex loved playing matchmaker. Hell, she was probably already plotting his wedding in that devious little mind of hers. He was the only bachelor left on the team. It didn't matter anyway because from hearing what Fred had told them, the last thing Campbell was looking for was a man. At least near term. Although Ace hadn't lied, Campbell was very attractive and did seem sweet.

"Alex...don't even go there." He warned playfully.

She laughed. "Oh, Diego. One day you're going to fall in love, and I'm going to plan that wedding of yours. You can't break tradition."

He groaned. "I'm hanging up now."

He heard her laugh before he ended the call. Before he could set the phone down, it rang. He thought it was Alex calling him back but was surprised to see it was Derek.

"Hello?"

"Hey, Diego. I just wanted to call and check-in and see how everything's going."

"We just got in a little while ago, and she's upstairs getting settled." He wasn't going to tell Derek about his snippiness. As Alex said, it would all be fine—he hoped.

"Good. I just got off the phone with Fred a little while ago. You guys were right. Someone was watching the diner. Shortly after you guys left, Fred noticed an unfamiliar vehicle with tinted windows pull into the vacant lot across the street, and it stayed there for a few hours. Nobody ever got out, but he could tell someone was there watching. He finally called the Sherriff. When he showed up, the driver said he was meeting someone. But as soon as the Sherriff left, Fred said the car pulled out and never showed back up."

"I think we got her out without anyone seeing her."

Derek chuckled. "Yeah. Fred told me that you smuggled her out in a seabag."

Diego grinned. It was pretty funny when they told Campbell to get inside the oversize bag. At first, she thought they were joking, but then Fred told her they weren't, and that it was the safest way to get her out without being seen. He could tell she wasn't thrilled about it. But in the end, it worked.

"Well, the important thing is that she's safe."

"That's true. How are you doing?"

Diego leaned his head back. "I'm hanging in there. The headaches were sporadic today. But they were manageable with some over-the-counter medicine. No double vision, so that was good."

"Good. Do you feel up to coming to the base tomorrow?"

He sat back up. "Really? I thought I wasn't allowed."

"I spoke with the Chain of Command and explained about some Intel that was shared with us that could possibly warrant a trip overseas in the coming weeks. And that the timeline fell in line with when you could possibly be cleared for duty. I asked them to permit you to partake in the in-person meetings and video calls relating to the operation."

"They actually said yes?"

"Well, Admiral Harlow said he didn't see any reason why you couldn't. He had asked how you were doing, and I told him that, in my opinion, I expected you to return in time for this mission, and it was important for you to be up to speed. I mean, there's nothing strenuous about sitting in a room and listening to people talk. He agreed."

Wow. That had shocked Diego, but he was grateful. Then his mind shifted to the woman upstairs.

"What about Campbell?" He asked.

"What about her?"

"Aren't I supposed to be watching her?"

"You don't have to play bodyguard. You're just providing her a secure place to lay low for the time being. That is all that's expected. She understands that."

"I'll go talk to her and let her know."

"Alright. Well then, I guess I'll see you tomorrow morning. Oh, and Dino said he'd swing by and pick you up."

Shit! That's right; he wasn't allowed to drive until he saw the doctor in a few days.

"Sounds good. I'll see you in the morning."

Diego disconnected the phone and stood up. He glanced at his watch. It was a little after six, and he wondered if Campbell was hungry. They had stopped at a drive-thru on the way, but that was hours ago, and she only ate a few chicken nuggets.

He climbed the stairs and went to her room. He knocked on the door and waited. When he didn't get an answer, he cracked the door. The small lamp on the table next to the bed gave the room a soft glow. He walked further into the room and found Campbell curled up sound asleep on the bed. He thought about waking her but decided against it. She looked peaceful, and he didn't want to disturb her. She'd been through a lot, and this was probably the first good night sleep she'd had in a while.

He saw the door to the closet was open and noticed she had put away all of the clothes that Alex had gotten her. She was very neat and organized. As he went to leave the room, he saw a notepad and pen lying on the bed. He didn't want her to roll over on it, so he picked it up and set it on the table next to the bed. He glanced at the page she had written on. And what she had written down brought a smile to his face. He could tell just from what she wrote that she was a very grateful person. It was like a to-do list, but it consisted of names, and next to the names was everything she wanted to thank the person for. He realized that every name on the list was everyone who played a part in helping her get out of town—Derek, Irish, Ace, Potter, Fred, Stella, himself, and even Alex for buying her clothes.

Just from some of the comments she'd made, it gave Diego the impression that she was a caring person. She definitely piqued his interest, and he couldn't wait to learn more about her.

CHAPTER SEVEN

The following day Campbell had woken when she heard Diego close his bedroom door and go downstairs. She thought about going down as well, but after he had snapped at her last night, she felt it was best to just stay in her room and out of his hair. After all, he was doing her a favor by letting her stay at his place. How many other people would welcome a total stranger into their home?

She looked around the spacious bedroom. She eyed the large window that had a custom built-in seat. She walked over, pulled back the curtains, and looked out the window. It faced a huge fenced back yard. It was just grass, but seeing that clean slate had her creative mind racing with ideas. Maybe as a trade-off, she'd offer some suggestions to him for the space.

She spent the next half hour making the bed and going through her routine of getting ready that included stretching out her leg, checking on her arms, and making sure they were healing. She walked into the large walk-in closet and looked through the clothes that Ace's fiancée dropped off. She couldn't believe the amount of clothes and toiletries she had bought her. She would definitely be repaying her when she had the opportunity to meet her. That was if she got to meet her. She picked out a pair of light wash jeans and a teal cotton long-sleeved t-shirt. She wanted to keep the marks on her arms hidden. Looking in the mirror, she changed her mind about leaving her hair down, so she threw it up into a ponytail.

She decided to take a chance and head downstairs. Since she missed dinner, she was a little hungry. When she got to the bottom of the stairs, the house was quiet. She walked around, looking for any sign of Diego.

"Hello?" She called out. "Diego?"

She walked through the house, but it was silent.

She looked out the front window and saw that his two cars were still parked in the driveway. She wondered where he could be. She checked the garage next, but that was dark.

What she really wanted was a cup of coffee, and she prayed he had some.

She loved his kitchen. If she had an opportunity to design one herself, she'd match his design to a "T."

Spotting the coffee maker, she made her way over to it and made a pot. She was glad to see he had an actual coffee maker with a pot. She wasn't a fan of the new fancy devices that many people fawn over. She loved hearing the sounds of the coffee brewing.

As she waited for the coffee to finish, she looked around the kitchen a little more. She wondered if Diego would mind if she cooked now and then. Although considering how upscale and customized the kitchen was, maybe he was a cook and wouldn't appreciate others in his kitchen.

She saw a piece of paper on the counter with her name on it. She looked at it and saw it was a note from Diego.

Campbell,

I didn't want to wake you, so I'm leaving this note. One of the guys drove me to work for a meeting.

Please make yourself at home. Also, the phone sitting next to this note is for you. It's preprogrammed with numbers. Mine is the first one. If for any reason you need something, call. If it is something important and I don't answer, keep going down the list until someone does. Someone will be able to find me. I also armed the home security system before I left. If you need out of the house, the alarm code is nine-five-two-six.

I'll try to give you a call sometime during the day.

Diego

She set the note down, then looked around. What in the hell was she supposed to do? She hated sitting around. Life was too short not to stay busy. At least at home, she had books, her tablet, or something to keep her occupied. Here she didn't have diddly squat.

With a sigh, she walked over to the coffee pot. She pulled a mug from the drainboard and poured herself a fresh cup of piping hot coffee. She took a sip and closed her eyes as the liquid hit her taste buds, bringing a smile to her face.

Taking her coffee with her, she walked into the living room, thinking maybe she'd watch some TV for a bit. She couldn't remember the last time she watched television. It had to have been when she was laid up in the hospital because there were no televisions in the guest house once she got home, and she wasn't going next door for a movie night with Mitchell. Plus, he wasn't much of a television person.

Her eyes landed on the small room that Diego had shown her last night. He had said he was going to make it into his office. She walked over to the room and flipped the light on. She ran her hands on the wall. They were smooth, sanded, and ready to be painted. Sitting in the corner, she eyed the paint cans, brushes, rollers, and floor covering.

Her dad had taught her a lot about construction, including painting. Unlike most people who despised the task, she loved it. At first, she was hesitant, not knowing if he would get upset, but after she debated it, she figured it was the least she could do to repay him for letting her stay.

She set her coffee down then hurried back to the kitchen to grab the phone Diego had left for her. She wanted it nearby in case he called. On the way back, she turned on the television and switched the channel to one of the music stations that played some dance tunes. As she moved her hips to the beat, she got to work.

"Thanks again for the ride today," Diego said to Dino as he grabbed his backpack and hopped out of the vehicle.

"No problem. I'll pick you up tomorrow at the same time."

"I'll be ready."

Diego was thankful that the Admiral allowed him to attend the meetings on base. Nobody really understood what it meant to a soldier to be included in team activities even when they technically weren't supposed to be. It sure beat sitting at home and dwelling on what the future held for his career. At least being around the guys improved his attitude a bit.

He shut the door and walked up toward the house. It was already starting to get dark. He didn't see any lights on inside the house. He felt bad for having to leave Campbell by herself all day, but when he called around mid-day to check in with her, she seemed fine and told him she was reading a book.

He unlocked the door and went to open it, but it wouldn't budge. He grinned, happy to see that Campbell was taking her safety seriously. He found the other key and inserted it into the top lock. When he heard the snick of the lock disengaging, he turned the knob and let himself in. Right away, he could smell fresh paint, and he wondered what it was from. He had a lot of paint sitting around the house, and he hoped that none of it had leaked or spilled.

He walked into the kitchen, flipped the light on, and set his bag on the counter. He wondered where Campbell was. The house was completely dark, except for the small plug-in lights in the kitchen and the living room near the staircase.

As he searched for Campbell and the source of the paint smell, he noticed the piece of paper on the counter by the small second sink located on the island.

Diego,

I hope you had a good day at work. I felt kinda useless just sitting around, so I thought I'd be a little productive myself and help you around the house since you were kind enough to open your home to me. Also, I found the stack of take-out menus next to the refrigerator and ordered dinner. I wasn't sure if you had eaten or not, and I didn't want to bother you, so I went ahead and ordered you something as well. There's an order of orange chicken, fried rice, and an egg roll in the refrigerator for you.

Campbell

He set the paper back down and looked around the house, wondering what she had done around the house. As he scanned the living room, his eyes landed on the closed door that led to the room he was making into his office. That door wasn't there when he left this morning. It had been sitting inside the room leaning up against the wall. *Had she hung it by herself? No way.*

He walked over, turned the knob, and the door opened perfectly. *Holy shit!* But soon, he realized where the paint fumes were coming from. He flipped on the light, and his jaw dropped in total amazement, seeing that the ceiling and walls had been painted perfectly. Hell, he couldn't have done a better job. It was quality work as if a professional had come in and done it. He looked around and noted that she had even cleaned everything up. There wasn't even a drop of paint on the hardwood floors. *Unbelievable.*

He climbed the stairs and went to her bedroom. He lightly knocked on the door. When she didn't answer, he tried the knob. When it turned, he slowly pushed the door open. He was shocked to see that she was sound asleep again. Though from the look of her position on the bed, she hadn't meant to fall asleep. He didn't want to wake her, but he also didn't want her to get cold. He saw the throw blanket draped over the back of the rocking chair on the other side of the room. He grabbed it and covered her with it. He grinned when he heard her light snores. She was out like a light, and again she looked peaceful.

Not wanting to stand around gawking at her in case she woke up, he slowly backed out of the room and closed the door behind him. He was bummed he wouldn't get to see her in the morning. Hopefully, they can catch up tomorrow evening.

CHAPTER EIGHT

"What the fuck do you mean she wasn't at the diner?" Mitchell shouted at Vinny through the phone. He couldn't believe what he was hearing. There had to be some mistake because there was no way in hell that Belle would try and pull a stunt like this—not after their last conversation. She knew what his expectations were and what the consequences would be if she didn't obey his orders.

"Exactly what I said, boss. She wasn't working. And the guy who owns the joint said he hasn't seen her since last week."

Mitchell pushed the chair back from the desk where he was sitting then stood up. He ran his hand through his hair before he began to pace. Where the hell could she have gone? She had pulled shit like this before, but she hadn't thought out her plan well because he found her within hours. But now it'd been over twenty-four hours.

"Are you sure you've checked everywhere?"

"Yes, and considering how small the town is and everyone knows her, it would be hard for her to hide and not be noticed."

Damn it! There wasn't much he could do since he was in Russia, four thousand seven hundred and thirty miles from home. Not to mention his flight wasn't scheduled for another three days, and there were limited flights from Arkhangelsk to St. Petersburg to catch a connecting flight back home.

"Fuck!" He was pissed. Everything he had done for her, and this was how she repaid him? He was done pussyfooting around. She would pay for this stunt when he found her.

"What do you want me to do?" Vinny asked.

Mitchell stared out the window overlooking the mining operation that would soon be half his. Once he signed the contract this evening at dinner, he would be the new co-owner of Delta Diamond Corporation, the parent company overseeing three major diamond mines in the Arkhangelsk Oblast region.

Nobody, not even Vinny, his closest confidant, knew why he was traveling to Russia. Just like nobody was aware that he had secretly put the West Virginia mine up for sale a few months ago.

He did that after he was tipped off that someone had filed a claim with the Mine Safety and Health Administration, disputing their initial accident investigation stemming from the accident that had killed Belle's dad, along with two other men. According to his source within the MSHA, the person submitted potentially damaging evidence, proving that the accidents over the last few years which resulted in several fatalities were, in fact, not accidents at all.

He already had a potential buyer, and if everything checked out, the sale was scheduled to go through in the next week or two. That way, he'd be long gone out of the country if the MSHA came back with a follow-up investigation. Even if anything came about, it would be nearly impossible for the U.S. to extradite him from Russia.

But now, Belle's disappearance put a wrench in his plan because she was part of it. Many of his associates would tell him not to even bother with her—that she was too much trouble. But he couldn't let her go. There was something about Belle that fascinated him. She had grace and elegance, not to mention her natural beauty. But what turned him on was her submissiveness. The first time he laid eyes on her, he knew she would belong to him. He remembered that fall day vividly as her dad introduced her to him. It was the day that he vowed to look at no other woman but her.

"Mitchell? Are you still there?" He heard Vinny ask.

He reached down and had to adjust himself. Just thinking about Belle got him hard.

"Keeping looking for her. I'll make a few calls to some folks that owe me favors. Someone knows something."

"Yes, sir. I'll be in touch."

Mitchell disconnected and threw his phone onto the desk. He turned to look out the window again. The ground was still covered in snow.

"Where are you hiding, Belle?" He mumbled to himself.

"Problem?" The male voice said from behind him.

When he turned, his friend and new business partner, Igor Vasiliev, stood in the doorway leading into the office.

Before taking over his father's business, Igor was a professional boxer claiming several national championships for Russia. He was in his late thirties, stood over six feet tall, and was ripped with muscles. He was always dressed to impress, and with his build, dirty blonde hair, and piercing blue eyes, the ladies gushed over him. But if he remembered correctly, Igor mentioned to him that he had a special lady in his life.

Mitchell gave him a half-smile. In conversation, he had mentioned Belle to Igor, but he didn't want to divulge that Belle was missing. Not yet. He'd let Vinny do some digging first."

"Just some business issues back at home. You know, tying up loose ends before I finalize the sale."

Igor grinned. "I do know. Selling a business entails a lot of paperwork. How's Belle doing? Is she excited about this new venture and moving here?"

Shit! He thought about lying but then thought otherwise. It wasn't wise to start a new business partnership by lying to your business partner. Maybe a half-truth statement would suffice.

"She's good. I actually haven't told her about our partnership yet. I was going to tell her once I got home. I wanted to have everything finalized before I told her."

Igor raised his eyebrows in surprise but then shrugged his shoulders. "It makes sense. With everything you've told me about her, I can't wait to meet her. Once you guys get settled here, we'll have to get together, and then we can introduce Mischa and Belle to one another."

Mitchell smiled. "That would be great. I'm sure Belle would love that."

Igor slapped his thighs before standing up. "Well, I'll get out of your hair for now. We're still meeting this evening for dinner, correct?"

Mitchell nodded. "Yes. I'm looking forward to meeting some of the management staff."

"Wonderful. I made reservations at the restaurant inside the hotel. That way, you don't have to bother with transportation."

"Thank you. I'll see you this evening."

Once Igor left the room, Mitchell glanced at his watch. He still had some time to make a few calls back home. His priority was finding Belle and making sure she understood that she would never leave him again.

CHAPTER NINE

Campbell woke up feeling a little sore, primarily through her arms and shoulders. She assumed it was from all the painting she had done. But it was worth it. She was happy with her work, and she hoped that Diego was both surprised and pleased.

She couldn't believe how quickly she had fallen asleep last night. She had all intentions of waiting up for Diego. Luckily, she had decided to leave him a note. After she ate her beef and broccoli and took a hot shower, she only meant to lay on the bed for a few minutes—not fall into a deep slumber. Her tiredness showed, considering she never once woke in the middle of the night, which had to have been a record for her. Ever since Mitchell started to get abusive, she had a hard time sleeping. Well, that was when he'd let her.

She pushed the plush blanket off her and rolled out of bed. Once she stood up, she stretched out her arms and back. It actually felt nice to get some exercise in, even though it consisted of painting.

As she bent over to give her legs a stretch, she felt a pinch of pain in her lower abdomen. She quickly stood up straight with her hand over the area where the pain was. "It's nothing," she muttered to herself. "I just overworked my muscles yesterday." While she was trying to convince herself that the slight bite of pain was nothing to worry about, uncertainties lurked around the edge of her subconscious as she remembered that was how her mom's issues began—a pain here and pain there. Then a few months later, she had been diagnosed with stage three ovarian cancer.

Shaking off the worry, she walked to the en-suite bathroom and continued going through her morning routine. Once she was dressed and ready to tackle the day, she headed downstairs in search of Diego. It felt like Deja vu when she got to the bottom of the stairs. The house was quiet. She looked out the window and saw both his vehicles were still parked in the driveway. She went to the door and saw the alarm was blinking red, meaning it was armed. She thought maybe he was still upstairs. Not knowing his sleeping habits, she decided to head to the kitchen to make a pot of coffee. That was when she saw another note. This time it was taped to the coffee maker. She grabbed it, and she felt her mood sour as she read it.

Campbell,

Sorry for another note. I was hoping to catch you last night, but you were already in bed when I got home. I guess reading that book yesterday really wore you out (kidding). Remind me tonight to thank the handywoman who painted my office and hung the door. Also, thank you for the Chinese food. It hit the spot after a long day. I shouldn't be late, so hopefully, we can catch up this evening. Again, if you need anything, don't hesitate to call.

Diego

She set the note down and grabbed the mug she used yesterday and poured herself a cup of coffee. She pulled a stool out and sat down at the island, wondering what she could do to occupy herself for the day.

She felt and heard her stomach growl. She noticed last night when she tried to find something to cook that Diego didn't have much food in the house. But she did remember seeing a bag of potatoes. She could make some home fries. She took a sip of her coffee before she got up and grabbed three small potatoes from the pantry. After setting the potatoes on the counter, she went into the living room to turn some music on. On her way back to the kitchen, she stopped at a shelving unit that held a bunch of various size picture frames. She smiled as she picked up the one frame containing a picture of Diego and a woman, she assumed was his mom. He was in his dress uniform. It was definitely an older picture because there was a significant difference in what he looked like then compared to what he looked like now. He definitely had a lot more muscle now, and she could even tell that his smile wasn't as bright now as it was back then. In the picture, the happiness from the day could be seen in his big smile and his eyes—those dark brown eyes of his sparkled.

She felt a slight pang in her belly as she thought about all the pictures she had of her and her family. She would love to have the opportunity to place them around a home she lived in and have those memories surrounding her. Even the ones that included her sister, Lizzy. Thankfully her pictures were some of the personal items she had been able to get packed up and stowed away in the storage unit without Mitchell knowing.

God, she wanted to give herself a swift kick in the butt for thinking about her sister. Campbell never saw her older sister's spiral of destruction coming. Lizzy, at one time, had a bright future ahead of her. She, too, was a dancer, and in Campbell's opinion, Lizzy was a better dancer. Lizzy had many ballet companies vying for her, and it was Lizzy's dream to dance for a major company. But that dream came to a screeching halt the day their mom was diagnosed with ovarian cancer. To this day, Campbell didn't know what had triggered Lizzy to go off the rails. It started slowly with Lizzy staying out all hours of the night and lying about where she had been. She started skipping her dance practices, and then before the family knew it, she had found herself involved with drug users. They all tried to help her, but the problem was that Lizzy didn't want help. The day their mom died was the last time Campbell had seen or spoken to her sister. She didn't even know where she was or if she was, even still alive. Her only hope was that one day she would reach out. Even though Mitchell had gotten her a new cell phone and number, Campbell kept her old phone just in case one day Lizzy would call.

Shaking off the memories, Campbell headed back into the kitchen. Her appetite had worn off, and she found herself no longer in the mood to eat. She put everything back where she found it, grabbed her cup of coffee, and went in search of something to keep her busy for the next couple of hours.

After meeting with Derek and going over some planning documents, Diego went in search of the guys. As he walked down the hall, he heard the sound of weights clanging together and knew where to head.

As he entered the gym, he saw Ace and Skittles lifting weights while Stitch and a couple of guys from Bravo Team were over on the mats doing various bodyweight exercises. His body felt the pull. For someone who was used to working out every day, it sucked not being able to—even if it was only temporary.

He eyed the pull-up bar, and Ace raised his eyebrow.

"Don't even think about it."

Diego shook his head then walked over to a bench that sat along the wall near the weight bench that Ace was on.

"This sucks," Diego said, and Ace chuckled.

"Come on, man. It hasn't even been a full week."

"I know, but I hate sitting around feeling helpless. It's just not who I am."

Ace put the weights down and grabbed his towel off the bar, then wiped the sweat from his face. He took a seat next to Diego.

"When do you see the doc again?"

"In a few days. Hopefully, he'll let me resume some physical activity."

"You said the double vision was gone, right?"

Diego nodded. "And the ringing in the ears. Thank God. That was driving me batshit crazy. The only symptom still lingering is the headaches. And those come and go and have different pain levels. It can be mild when one comes on, but then sometimes it can hurt like a bitch."

"Minus the headaches, it sounds like you're progressing."

He shrugged his one shoulder. "I guess so."

"How was Campbell's first day?"

Diego scratched his head and chuckled. "I guess okay."

Ace gave him a funny look. "You guess?"

"I haven't seen her since she went to bed the day we got her to the house."

"What?"

"By the time I got home last night, she was already asleep. But she had good reason to be."

"Why is that?"

Diego chuckled. "You aren't going to believe this. You know the room downstairs, off the living room that I was planning on making my office?"

"Yeah."

"Well, it was painted from top to bottom, and the door was hung."

Ace's eyes widened. "She did all that?"

"Sure as shit did."

"Wow! Did you know she could do that?"

"While I was showing her around, she mentioned how her dad had taught her a few things, but damn, I was blown away. It looked like a professional had done it. It was that good."

Ace laughed. "I wonder what finished project you'll go home to tonight?"

"Who knows. I just hope that I get to see her."

Ace grinned. "Do you?"

Diego realized how that sounded. "Don't be going all Alex on me."

Ace barked out a loud laugh that got Skittles and Stitch's attention. They came over to see what was so funny, and Ace told them. They, too, thought it was funny.

"Mia was asking me about her last night. Apparently, the girls were talking about it on the group chat last night," Stitch told them.

"I know. Anna Grace brought her up this morning and asked if I knew anything about her," Skittles said.

"Well, I'm sure that Alex is planning some sort of welcome party for her," Ace said with an eye roll.

It made Diego laugh, but it also didn't surprise him. That was just how the ladies were—friendly and caring.

"Yeah, well, remember Campbell's supposed to be lying low." Diego reminded them.

"Oh, you just want to keep her locked in the house, so she'll finish all the projects," Ace said, sounding amused, then explained to Stitch and Skittles what she did to Diego's office.

Moments later, they were joined by Joker and Playboy from Bravo Team. They were wondering what all the laughter was about, and Ace retold the story.

"Damn. Pretty and handy. When do we get an introduction?" Playboy teased, and Joker laughed.

Diego looked at both of them with a serious expression. "She's off-limits."

Joker held his hands up as if he was surrendering. "Hey, don't look at me. Playboy was the one who said it."

"Dude, I was just kidding," Playboy said, giving his teammate the stink eye.

Joker laughed it off but then sobered, looking at Diego. "Seriously though, if you need anything, just let us know. You know we've got your back."

Diego nodded. "Thanks. I appreciate it."

After Playboy and Joker said their goodbyes, that just left Diego, Ace, and Skittles. Diego looked at his watch and noticed it was after four. He wanted to get home before Campbell fell asleep.

He looked at Skittles. "Hey, do you mind giving me a ride home?"

"No. Give me a few minutes to grab my things."

"Thanks. I'll meet you out at your truck."

Skittles left the room, and Diego looked at Ace and Stitch. "Since there are no meetings planned for tomorrow, I'll be at the house if you need anything."

Everyone stood up, preparing to leave.

"Maybe, we'll stop by tomorrow after work. Derek said we might have a shortened day."

"Cool. Just give me a call."

"Will do."

They all said their goodbyes, promising to see each other tomorrow.

CHAPTER TEN

Diego entered the house through the garage. Again, like the night before, all the lights were off downstairs, and he thought he might have missed Campbell again. But the glow from the television in the living room caught his eye.

As he came through the kitchen, he saw the pizza box on the counter. He lifted the top of the box, and his stomach rumbled as the aroma of the meat lovers and green peppers hit his nose. He hadn't eaten since lunch and could go for some chow. He dropped his bag by the laundry room door before heading into the living room.

Curled up in the corner of the couch was Campbell. Again, she was fast asleep and looked like an angel. The volume on the TV was low, but Diego could tell it was one of those sappy love stories on the *Hallmark* channel. His sisters and mom loved those movies.

Looking back down at Campbell, his eyes roamed over her body. She was tiny. She had a pair of dark grey yoga pants, and his eyes widened when he realized she was wearing an old t-shirt of his he had in the laundry room for when he was working around the house. She had the bottom tied in a knot at her waist, and to see her in something of his hit a part of him deep inside. With her hair pulled back in a ponytail, his eyes made contact with the bruise that was still noticeable along her cheek, and he felt the anger grow within him. No woman deserved to be a man's punching bag. Neither Diego, nor any of the others tolerated that shit.

Shaking off the feeling, he saw the top of her arms had speckles of grey paint along her skin, and he immediately looked around, wondering what else she had done around the house. Not that he was complaining, because she was damn good at painting. He did see the nail gun, a box of nails, and a tube of caulk lying by the office door. *No, she did not,* he thought to himself. He had already precut the trim and baseboards. They just needed to be painted then installed.

He walked over and opened the door and was once again blown away. All the trim around the door, closet, and windows were up, along with the baseboard. He was in awe of her talent. *Fucking amazing!*

When he returned to the living room, he wondered where she had painted. There were only a few rooms left that needed to be done, and those were the bedrooms upstairs. Curious, he climbed the stairs. When he opened the first door, the fumes from the paint hit him. He flipped the light on and stood in the doorway in amazement. Again, she had painted the ceiling and walls as if she did this for a living.

He turned the light off, closed the door, and headed back downstairs, thinking of ways he could repay her generosity. He didn't want her to think she had to help him around the house—she was a guest in his home for Pete's sake, though she was incredibly good at what she did.

As he quietly passed by the couch, he took another glance at her, and something caught his eye that he hadn't noticed earlier. *Are those ice packs smooshed between her arms?* He leaned closed to look, and he confirmed they were ice packs. Shit. He hoped she hadn't hurt herself while painting, or worse, with the nail gun. He didn't want to wake her, but he wanted to be sure that she was alright.

He gently ran his hand up and down her thigh while calling her name in a low voice.

Campbell was having the most incredible dream. She was standing on a beach as the ocean's waves crashed near her feet. In the distance, she could see a man walking towards her. As he approached, she was able to get a better look at him. He was tall, had a muscular build, and a shaved head. She couldn't see his face; for some reason, that feature was blurred out. It was odd. He looked very familiar. He stepped in front of her, and she tilted her head back to look at him. The sun blinded her from seeing his face.

"Campbell." Her name rolled off his tongue in a deep but whispered voice.

She continued to stare, and he repeated her name. Suddenly, his face started to appear, and she gasped as his hand cupped her cheek.

"Diego?" She uttered under her breath.

"Yes, Campbell, it's me."

Her outer leg began to feel warm, as if someone was caressing it. The warmth spread lower toward the area below her knee—the mangled portion of her leg, and she jerked away. *No!* She didn't allow anyone to see the damage done to her.

The guy repeated her name—this time in a loud, forceful tone.

"Campbell!"

Suddenly, everything in her dream faded to black, and she jerked awake. She flung her body upward as her eyes popped open, and her heart raced. She focused her eyes, and the first thing she saw was Diego's concerned expression and dark chocolate eyes staring at her.

"Diego?" She asked, wanting to be clear she still wasn't dreaming.

He smiled and caressed her cheek. The touch was identical to the one in her dream.

"Yeah, Campbell. It's just me."

She lifted her arm to tuck a few strands of her unruly hair behind her ear, when suddenly Diego's gorgeous smile slowly turned upside down. His eyes were laser-locked onto her arms—her ugly arms that would most likely be scarred for life.

After finishing working upstairs, her arms were in pain and looked a little red and swollen, so she took some over-the-counter pain medicine and put some ice on them before laying down on the couch to rest. She hadn't intended to fall asleep.

"What the hell?" Diego yelled out as she panicked and tried grabbing the throw on the back of the couch to cover the injury, but it was too late. He had seen them.

"Don't you dare," he told her in a deep stern voice.

She looked up at him. There were tears in her eyes. She didn't want him to see what Mitchell had done to her. She didn't want anyone to see the abuse she tolerated.

"Please...don't look at them," she whispered and lowered her head. She couldn't even look at him. She didn't want to see the pity.

She felt the couch dip next to her and knew he sat down.

"Campbell, look at me," he said in a calm and soothing tone as he cupped her chin and tilted her face towards his. "Let me see," he told her, but she shook her head as a tear slipped from her eye.

Campbell kept eye contact with him, and she felt him pull back the throw blanket, revealing the scabbed over cuts and bruising along her forearms.

He glanced down. "This isn't good. We need to make sure these wounds stay clean." His care and compassion brought more tears to her eyes.

"I've been washing them." She told him, hoping that he would accept that and let it go.

"No, baby. These are more than just basic cuts. Some look pretty deep. Did you have anyone look at them before?"

She shook her head as another tear fell from her eye. "No."

His face took on an angry expression, and his eyes darkened. "Why the hell not?" He questioned as he kept her arm in his hand.

She didn't want to answer that question. She was already embarrassed that he saw her wounds. She could only imagine what he'd think when she told him that Mitchell said she would be fine and that the scars would be a reminder for her to listen the next time.

"Campbell?" He repeated her name, and she looked into his eyes. He had beautiful eyes with thick black eyelashes. "You should've had someone look at these. I'll be right back," he said before he stood then walked into the kitchen. She heard him talking to someone on the phone. Minutes later, he came back into the room, set his phone on the table, and sat back down on the coffee table in front of her.

"Okay, Stitch is going to stop by and take a look. I trust him with my life."

"Who's Stitch?" She questioned. She didn't want more people to know her business.

"He's one of my teammates. We'll see what he says, though just from looking at the scabs, you probably should've gotten stitches."

"I tried to take care of it myself," she told him honestly.

He gently squeezed her hand. "From now on, you don't have to do things by yourself. We're all here to help you. Okay?"

She nodded.

"Did this happen during the same altercation when you got that bruise on your cheek?" He asked, appearing to bite the inside of his cheek.

She nodded again before lowering her eyes.

"Hey," he said, tilting her chin up. She met his eyes. "Remember, all of this is in the past."

"I know. It's just embarrassing."

"Can I ask you something?" He still held her hand.

"Sure."

"Why did you stay? Fred told us some, but not a lot, because he said you wouldn't tell him what was actually happening at home."

She thought about his question but then answered honestly. "Fear."

"Fear of what?" He pressed.

"Of what he would do next."

He wanted to ask another question, but then there was a knock at the front door. Before he got up to answer it, he leaned forward and kissed her forehead. She almost fainted when his firm, warm lips gently touched her skin. "We'll talk more later."

She swallowed hard as she watched him walk to the door.

Stitch finished cleaning the open wounds with antiseptic wipes.

Campbell liked him. He appeared less intimidating than the others she had already met. He told her about his wife Mia and how she was a veterinarian and had her own clinic, along with a rescue shelter she ran with Skittles' wife, Anna Grace. Campbell loved animals and had always wanted a pet, but her parents would never let her get one. Maybe someday.

"How old are you?" Stitch asked her as he started to wrap her lower left arm with a gauze wrap. Thankfully, her right arm didn't need to be covered.

"That isn't a nice question to ask a lady," she replied with a small smile on her lips. Stitch's cheeks turned red, and he laughed. "You got me there. Sorry. That was rude of me."

"It's okay. I won't hold it against you. And for the record, I'm twenty-five." She admitted, and he smiled.

"No offense, but you look like you're about nineteen or twenty."

"I hear that quite often."

He stood up. "Well, I think you're all set. I don't see anything that shows an infection setting in. You were smart enough to keep them clean, though you probably could've used a few stitches. I can't promise that you won't have some scarring."

"It'll just go along with the others," she mumbled under her breath. But apparently, she said it a little louder than she intended.

"What was that?" Diego asked, and she snapped her head up. When she didn't answer, he asked her again. "What did you just say?"

She shook her head and looked away. "Nothing." When she glanced at Stitch, he stood there with his arms crossed in front of his chest. The smile he wore just minutes ago was replaced with a scowl. He must've heard her too. She didn't want to continue this conversation, so she decided it was a good time to call it a night. She stood up.

"Stitch, thank you again for coming over and taking care of this," she told him as she held up her arms. "It was also nice meeting you."

He nodded his head. "It was nice meeting you as well. I'll come by in a few days to have a look again to make sure they're healing properly."

"Thanks." She then turned toward Diego. He was standing in a similar stance as Stitch, though he appeared angrier. "I'm going to head upstairs and turn in for the night. There's pizza on the counter if either of you would like any." She offered before walking toward the stairs.

"I'll see you tomorrow morning." He told her, which surprised her, considering he had been going into work.

She turned around. "You will?" She asked.

"I have some things around here to do. I can't let the construction fairy do all the work." He winked and gave her a sexy smirk. She felt warmth in her cheeks as she tried to hide her smile.

"I guess I'll see you tomorrow then. Goodnight."

Diego watched Campbell climb the stairs. When he heard her say that about her scars, it had pissed him off. He wanted to press her on what she meant when she said that the scars would just go along with others.

Once she was out of earshot, Stitch didn't waste any time. "What the fuck did she mean when she said those scars will match the others?"

Diego bit the inside of his cheek and shook his head. "I have no clue, but I'm gonna find out."

Stitch ran his hand through his short brown hair. "Seeing those marks on her arms gave me flashbacks from Afghanistan."

Diego agreed. The last time either of them had seen anything like that was when Alex was kidnapped, and her captors had taken a whip to her back. He still got chills remembering the video footage. It was something he vowed never to watch again.

"I was getting her to open up a bit right before you got here. She said it was fear that kept her there."

"I feel so bad for her. I mean, having no family and then being stuck in an abusive relationship when it appeared she really had no way out."

"Well, she's out now, and I intend to make sure it stays that way."

Diego slapped his back. "You hungry? I think she ordered meat lovers with green peppers."

"You had me at meat." Stitch teased and walked with him into the kitchen.

As he and Stitch ate and talked, Diego was making a list of questions in his head to ask Campbell tomorrow. Since he didn't have to go to the base, she'd be in his company all day.

CHAPTER ELEVEN

Campbell and Diego were enjoying the afternoon together. He had been caught off guard when his doctor called first thing in the morning and asked to see him. At first, he thought something was wrong, but the doctor settled his nerves when he told him that he would be out of the office on the day he was supposed to come in for his scheduled appointment.

His doctor had been pleased with the progress he'd made so far and cleared him to resume light activities. He still wasn't supposed to do anything strenuous. The doctor said his headaches could continue for a few more weeks but didn't see any long-term effects hindering his return to active-duty status.

The doctor also gave him some home remedies to combat the headaches in place of over-the-counter medicines, such as; going to a quiet place or going outside and getting fresh air, or lying down and turning off the lights. Another suggestion was to put a cold or hot pack on his neck or head. The last one was to do some deep breathing and relaxation exercises. He'd rather do any of those the doctor recommended than take medication.

On the way home, he stopped at the local donut shop and brought home a dozen of the most amazing donuts he ever had. They were cake donuts with custom toppings. Apparently, Campbell loved them too. She was on her third one. It was a banana pudding donut, topped with whipped cream and a dab of banana pudding in the middle of the whipped cream, with a nilla wafer to top it off.

She popped the last bite in her mouth before wiping the crumbs from her face. She had a little bit of whipped cream stuck on the corner of her mouth, and without even thinking, he reached over and wiped it with his thumb.

She stilled and stared at him. He watched as her pupils dilated before his eyes. *Was she feeling the same attraction as he?* He wondered.

Not wanting to stare and make her uncomfortable, he grinned. "Sorry, you had a little bit of whipped cream there." He said as he wiped it on his jeans, although he would've rather licked it. Jesus, he needed to tamp down his excitement before he completely embarrassed himself.

Focusing on the project in front of him, he picked up the nail gun. Now that he'd been cleared to resume light activities, together, he and Campbell began installing the baseboard and trim in the upstairs bedroom that she had painted yesterday.

As Campbell knelt next to him, holding the board in place, he had to stop himself from leaning towards her. Whatever fruity-scented lotion or perfume she wore was enticing, and it drove him crazy.

After the piece was nailed to the wall, she turned and picked up the next board. They only had two more to go, and they'd be done. The guys were supposed to come by and help him move the boxes of tiles and buckets of Thin-Set Mortar for the bathroom connecting two of the bedrooms upstairs. They were also going to help him move the sections of fence and posts he had delivered.

She handed him the next piece. For the most part, they worked in silence with some music playing. He hadn't brought up last night's ordeal, and she never spoke of it either. He did notice that she wore a long-sleeved t-shirt.

She handed him the next piece. He lined it up, and she held it in place while he secured it. They repeated that same sequence one more time. When the last board was in place, they both stood and looked at their work. The large windows offered a gateway for light to filter into the room. He couldn't wait to get it furnished, to see the final look.

He turned to Campbell as she stood there looking at the progress.

"I never got a chance to thank you in person for the work you've done around here."

She smiled and shrugged her shoulders. "It was something to keep me busy."

"You're very talented."

"Thank you."

"So, what type of furniture and décor do you think should go in here?" He asked her.

She looked at him. "Did you have anything in mind?"

He chuckled. "No. I would probably end up asking Alex or one of the others for their opinion. But since you're here and you helped, I want you to decorate it."

Her eyes widened. "What if you don't like my suggestion?"

He grinned. "I'm pretty sure I'll like any ideas you have."

She nibbled on her lip as she looked around the room. "Well, what about adding some navy blue for an accent color?"

He smiled. "I used that color in my room."

"Oh." She walked toward the window then turned before scanning the room one more time. "How about a bold yellow? With the natural light that these big windows offer, it would be perfect."

He nodded. "I like it."

Just as he was about to say something else, the doorbell rang. It must've startled Campbell because he saw her flinch.

"It's okay. It's probably the guys. They were coming over to help me move some things."

"Oh."

He removed his toolbelt then took her hand. "Come on. I'll introduce you to the ones you haven't met yet."

She dug her heels into the floor and wouldn't move. When he faced her, he could see the hesitation, but he wasn't letting her hide. She needed to get used to being around people, especially the guys.

Diego ran his palms down her arms. "Remember Campbell; we're the good guys. We're here to protect you, and we're also your friends now. I know is it's probably hard to let your guard down considering we can all be pretty intimidating, but can you try. I swear to you that none of us would ever hurt you."

She looked at him then licked her lips. "Okay."

He grinned and squeezed her hand.

Campbell stood back and watched as the guys helped Diego move the materials that needed to be relocated to the garage. Of course, she stood by, making sure Diego didn't try to pick up any of the items, though she was convinced that the guys would rip his ass if he attempted to.

She had to admit that the men were friendly, even those she met for the first time today. She enjoyed listening to them rag on one another in a joking manner.

She looked at her watch and was surprised when she saw how late it was. It was almost five o'clock. Where had the time gone?

Stitch approached her, and she smiled.

"How are the arms today?" He asked, keeping his voice low so the others wouldn't hear.

She smiled. "They're good." She pulled the sleeves up to show him that she changed the gauze wrap on one arm.

He winked, then Diego joined them. "We're going to go hang on the back patio for a bit. You're welcome to join us if you'd like."

"That's okay. I'll let you spend some time with your friends. I think I might take a load off for a little bit."

He stared at her for a few seconds, then nodded his head.

"If you change your mind, you know where we'll be."

She smiled. "I know. Enjoy your friends."

She watched Diego and Stitch go out the back door. She wished she had friends like that. She felt her stomach growl. She wasn't sure what Diego's plans were for dinner. Maybe she'd just look for something to nibble on until the guys left. She opened the refrigerator and saw that he had a few bags of various lunchmeats, along with some fixings to make sandwiches. She wondered if the others were hungry.

Ten minutes later, she had two platters loaded with roast beef and turkey sandwiches, along with two bags of potato chips.

She took them out to the guys. They were shocked but very grateful.

"Thank you, Campbell. This looks delicious," Skittles told her as he bit into a turkey sandwich. The others followed suit and thanked her before devouring their sandwiches.

She was about to go back inside when Diego stopped her. "Why don't you sit outside with us for a little while?"

She didn't want to appear non-sociable, so she pulled up a chair next to Diego. She sat and listened to them talk about their kids and wives. She learned that Frost and his wife were expecting a baby in a few weeks. It was interesting to learn about the men behind the armor they wore. Thankfully, they didn't ask her many personal questions.

"Speaking of babies, you're coming to the baby shower next week, right?" Frost asked Diego.

"Shit! With everything happening, I totally forgot about it. What time?"

"Not this Saturday, but next Saturday, six o'clock at Bayside."

"Count me in."

Frost looked at Campbell. "You'll come with Diego, won't you?"

The surprise invitation caught her off guard. "Umm..."

"You have to come," Irish told her. "Our women are dying to meet you."

Her eyes widened, and she knew she looked frightened, and she wondered why these women she heard so much about would want to meet her. She was a nobody—just a woman looking to start her life over.

"Dude, I think you're scaring her." She heard the one guy say. Dino, that was his name. He was married to Arianna, and they had a dog, Nigel.

She needed to overcome the fear and just let go. If she truly wanted to move on with her life and live freely, she would need to learn to trust people. Somewhere in the back of her mind, she knew that not everyone was filled with an evil soul.

Diego held his hand out, and she looked at it before looking into his eyes. It was as if he could read her mind.

"Take the chance, Campbell; we'll catch you if you fall. I promise you that."

She looked up at him and then around at the others. None of them had done anything to make her fearful, and they were trying to be friendly and include her.

Her mouth and throat felt dry. She reached for Diego's soda off the table and took a drink. Once she felt she could speak, she answered.

"Okay. But can we do this my way?" She could see the questions in each of their eyes, so she elaborated. "I'm not a very sociable person, although I think that may change hanging around you guys." She smiled, and they chuckled.

"What do you have in mind?" Diego asked her.

"Could we do a dinner here first at the house?" She looked at the others. "Would you all come over for dinner? You and your families?"

"Hell, honey, one thing you'll learn around us is that we never turn down a home-cooked meal." Potter teased and offered her a small smile.

She smiled back, then glanced at Diego, who also had a big smile on his face.

"How about Saturday around eighteen hundred?" He asked the guys, and they all agreed. She wrinkled her forehead. She knew that was military time, but she didn't know the times off the top of her head. She looked down at her hands lying in her lap and started to count the hours on her fingers.

Diego leaned over; his lips were right next to her ear. She could feel his warm breath against her skin. "That's six o'clock." He whispered.

Slowly she turned her head and locked gazes with him. He winked at her, and it was at that moment she was aware there was something brewing between the two of them.

❧

Once the guys left, Campbell and Diego went to their rooms to get cleaned up.

Diego pulled on a pair of track pants, then a long-sleeved t-shirt. He and Campbell had opened the windows earlier because it had been so lovely out, but now it was a little chilly. That was the problem with spring weather—you never knew what you were going to get. Not until one day it made it into the high eighties or nineties and stayed there throughout summer.

While he finished up, he kept reminiscing from earlier when he and Campbell were working in the bedroom. He honestly enjoyed her company, which was odd because usually, he preferred to work alone, unless it was a big job that required two or more people to accomplish it.

As he walked down the stairs, he saw Campbell standing in the living room by the shelving unit, looking at the pictures of his family. His heart suddenly ached for her. She had been robbed of her family.

He walked closer, and she turned around and smiled at him. It wasn't a smile that reached her eyes—it was more of a smile of envy, and he completely understood. She held in her hand one of his favorite pictures. It was him with his entire family. It had been taken at a reunion a few years ago. By luck, he was home and not deployed and was able to attend.

"You have a big family. They look happy."

He smiled at her. He was proud of his family. "I do. We're very close."

"That has to be hard on you and them, considering your job and not being able to see them much."

"It is. But they understand. And for me, being a SEAL was my choice."

"Did you always want to be a SEAL?"

He snickered. "No. I enlisted in the Navy because I just wanted to serve my country. I figured it would be an easy way to see the world. But during basic training, I was picked to take the SEALs PST."

"What's a PST?"

"Physical Screening Test. The Navy has a physical readiness test that all personnel must meet. But the SEALs have their own, which is the PST."

"Is it hard? I mean, what does it consist of?"

"You have to complete so many push-ups, sit-ups, pull-ups, not to mention there is a timed mile and half run, along with a timed five-hundred-yard swim."

"Wow!"

"Yeah. Many people think it sounds easy, but it's harder than it seems once you start the evolution. After boot camp, I was put into a program called BUD/S Prep. There I learned about the Special Warfare communities. I also started an extensive physical training program that lasted for seven weeks. The prep program is designed to help candidates get into better shape before heading to BUD/S."

"BUD/S—that's where you go through hell week, and there's also a bell there that if you ring it, it signifies that you're dropping out, right?"

He grinned. "That's right." He said, and she smiled.

"You know, you are even more beautiful when you smile." He told her, and she lowered her eyes. He wasn't sure if she was embarrassed by his compliment or if it had upset her.

"Hey, I didn't say that to upset you." He said, lifting her chin. "You really do have a beautiful smile, and you should use it more."

"Where I come from, there isn't anything to smile about. I don't think I've smiled in the last year to a year and a half until I came here.

"Come on. You had to have smiled to get tips at the diner."

What she told him next put things in perspective for him.

"It is easy to fake a smile and put on a show to let the outside world think everything is great, when in reality it's the complete opposite." She walked over to the table and picked up the bottle of water she had sat there earlier. She played with the label on the bottle of water. "Until you and your friends got me off that mountain, my life had sucked. It hadn't always been that way. It all started when I lost my mom to ovarian cancer. Then when my dad died, I felt lost. I was numb. As I told you and the guys earlier, I'm not a social butterfly, so I didn't bat an eye when Mitchell showed up out of the blue. He was someone I knew and trusted at that time. I just hadn't known that I was going to be sucked into Satan's lair to be controlled by him."

Campbell sat down on the couch, and he sat next to her.

"Damn. I'm sorry you had to go through all of that alone."

She shrugged her shoulders as she brought her legs up onto the couch and tucked them under her.

"It's okay."

He shook his head. "It's not okay. You don't deserve the curve balls life has thrown at you."

She stared at him. "At least you know now why I seem a little standoffish, but please know it's nothing against you. I appreciate everything you've done for me. I'm sure it's awkward for you to open up your home to a complete stranger."

"I'm glad I could help, and I'm glad we were in a position to get you out of that mess."

She smiled. "I'm glad too. I don't know how I'll ever repay you for your kindness."

He grinned. "You can repay me by opening up that beautiful heart of yours and living the life you deserve. And, you can have dinner with me." He winked, then reached over to the table next to the couch and picked up a stack of menus. "What will it be tonight—Italian, Chinese, subs, or burgers?"

She smiled. "How about a home-cooked meal?"

He gave her a sideways look and smirked. "A home-cooked meal sounds delicious, but have you seen the pantry and refrigerator? I don't eat at home often, and when I do, it's microwave meals or take-out."

"Well, if you're up for it, how about we go to the grocery store so I can pick up a few things, then I'll cook for us."

"I think that sounds amazing. Come on, let's go."

After dinner, Diego helped her clean up before he excused himself to make a call. Even if it was just steak, baked potatoes, and salad, Campbell was one hell of a cook. The attention to detail she put into the meal made it feel and taste like he was dining at a five-star restaurant. He was even more impressed with the way she moved around the kitchen and multitasked. She practically had the kitchen spotless before they even sat down to eat.

He was sitting in his recliner watching a baseball game on TV while scrolling through his phone. He came across a message from his mom. She was planning a big party for his dad's birthday in two weeks, and she wanted to see if there was any way he could make it. He thought about it.

From what his doctor said, it would most likely be another two to three weeks before he would stand in front of the review board. Maybe he could make it as long as he was cleared to fly.

Just as he was setting his phone down, Campbell walked into the living room, carrying a glass of root beer and a book. He found out that root beer was her favorite soda flavor. He ended up buying her three, twelve packs.

She took a seat on the couch at the end closest to him. He found himself watching her as she curled into a ball and got comfortable. He wanted to hear more from her about her life. Hell, he wanted to know everything.

As if sensing his gaze, she turned her head in his direction.

"You know, staring at someone is creepy."

"Tell me a little about this Mitchell guy."

She stared at him then set her book down on the table. "What do you want to know? I thought Fred would've told you guys everything."

"He didn't go into detail. He was mainly focused on the plan to get you out."

"Mitchell is like the devil. He manipulates you until he has you in his grasp and knows that you can't function without him."

"I don't mean to sound insensitive in asking this, but your limp—is that because of him?"

She looked at him as if she was surprised he asked. She'd learn that he didn't beat around the bush when he wanted to know something.

She picked up her glass and took a drink before she cleared her throat.

"I had just gotten home from an audition at a dance company in Cleveland. Mitchell hadn't been happy that I went. He didn't want me dancing. He told me so."

"When he confronted me about how it went, and I told him the company presented an offer to me, he completely lost it. He told me flat out that I wasn't leaving him for a dance career." She laughed sarcastically. "Honestly, I would've left him if I was offered a job to scrape gum off sidewalks. It didn't matter; I just wanted out."

She played with the ends of her long hair—twirling it around her finger. It was a sign of nervousness or anxiousness. Diego could tell she didn't like rehashing her past. The last thing he wanted was for her to feel uncomfortable.

"Campbell, we don't have to talk about it if it upsets you."

"No. It's okay. And to be honest, I haven't told anyone what happened."

"What? Why?"

She took another drink. "Because it's hard to press charges against someone who practically has the whole town in their back pocket."

"Anyway, he and I got into a screaming match, and it turned physical. He told me that one way to keep me from going was if I couldn't dance anymore. I didn't understand what he meant until he picked up a baseball bat and started swinging it. I tried to run, but I tripped and fell. He proceeded to bash my leg until Vinny stepped in and stopped him. Thank goodness my leg was the only thing broken. Vinny drove me to the hospital. By the time I got there, I had gone into shock from the pain. For the first few days, it was touch-and-go on whether I'd lose the lower half of my leg."

Diego swallowed hard. "Jesus Christ. I'm sorry you had to go through that. I'm sure the recovery was excruciating."

She nodded. "It was. I spent months in the hospital. But that was okay because that meant I didn't have to live under his roof."

"What did you tell the doctors happened to you?"

"I lied. I told them that while I was out hiking, I was hit by falling rocks. It's not uncommon in the mountains. Vinny validated my story. I hated lying, but there was no point in telling the truth when I knew that nothing would come of it."

"Why did you go back to him afterward? You can never heal yourself if you keep going back to what broke you to begin with."

"I had a lot of time to think while I was laid up in the hospital. First, I knew I didn't have anywhere else to go. I didn't have much money. So I started to lay out a plan. I agreed with Mitchell that the only way I'd come back was if I moved back into the guest house until he showed me that he truly had changed. And he had to quit drinking, which surprisingly he did. I just needed a few months to get some things done."

She played with the rim of her glass. "It's funny, you know. I was planning on leaving town the day you guys showed up. I hadn't intended to work that day. I just came to the diner to say goodbye to Fred and Stella. I couldn't leave without seeing them. They both have been so supportive and helpful through my ordeal. I just wish I could've been honest with them."

"If you don't mind me asking, what happened to your dad? Fred said something about a mining accident."

Diego saw a shift in her expression. She pressed her lips together tightly and looked away for a quick second. He wondered what triggered that reaction.

"I'm not fully convinced that my dad was killed in an *accident*." Diego noticed how she emphasized the word accident.

"Why do you say that?"

"My dad loved being a coal miner. I know it wasn't the most glamorous job, but he enjoyed it. His dad and grandfather were miners as well. When my mom died, my older sister, Lizzy, went crazy."

That was news to Diego. Fred never said anything about a sister.

"You have a sister?" He asked.

She rolled her eyes out of frustration. "Yeah, but don't ask me where she is. She was walking on a tight rope a few months before Mom died. In my opinion, I don't think she knew how to cope with watching Mom wilt away day-by-day, so she turned to alcohol and drugs. When Mom finally passed, Lizzy packed her things and moved out. The sad part was that she never even said goodbye. Dad had taken me to my dance practice, and when we got home later that evening, she was gone. That was a little over five years ago. I haven't heard a peep from her. I don't even know if she's still alive."

"Damn, I'm sorry about that, and hearing about your mom and dad."

She gave him a soft smile. "Thanks. Anyway, a few months before my dad's accident, he started acting differently."

"How so?"

"He became quiet and distant from most of the guys he worked with. We lived in an apartment complex that Mitchell also owned. Most of the men and women who worked at the mine were tenants as well. He mentioned a few times that he was looking at another company, and that we could be moving again." She looked down at her lap, and Diego understood why. Her father had died before that could happen.

"I knew the dangers of working in a mine, and so did my dad. Numerous things could go wrong. But you always think it would never happen to you or anyone you know. I remember that day like it was yesterday. I was still going to school as well as dancing. I had just gotten home when there was a knock on the door. It was Leonard, my dad's friend, and our neighbor. As soon as I saw his face, I knew he wasn't going to deliver good news. After that, it felt like the next month had just blended all together."

"I was a grieving twenty-three-year-old who had just lost the most important person in her life at the time. Mitchell knew that and took advantage of my vulnerability. He swooped in like the hero and offered me the guest house on his property. I had nowhere else to go. My dad was the money maker. I was a college student and dancer."

"When did you and Mitchell become romantically involved?" Just saying that left a bad taste in Diego's mouth.

"At first, he played the caring friend. He took care of all of the funeral arrangements and costs. I was never interested in dating anyone. I was more focused on making a name for myself in school and dancing. But he finally won me over. And what a huge mistake that was. We began dating, but after a few months is when I began to see a change in him. He started drinking more and became verbally abusive. He loved to throw parties for his friends and would make me be the hostess. I tried to get out of the relationship, but then he'd pull the "you owe me" card. He would carry on about everything he had done for me over the two years that followed my dad's death. I felt like I was stuck. I attempted to leave a couple of times, but he tracked me down and forced me back into his twisted world. I swear the man had a LoJack system installed on me. But the final straw was my leg. Again, I couldn't legally do anything since it was his word against mine and knowing who he had on his side; it wasn't worth the fight. The Sherriff was on my side, and even though I never said a word about Mitchell taking a baseball bat to my leg, he knew and felt awful."

Diego was furious. The more he heard, the more pissed off he became. But he tamped down his anger because the last thing he wanted to do was scare Campbell.

"So the fucker gets a free pass?" He asked with a little bite to his words.

"Pretty much."

"That's fucked up."

"It is. But Fred always promised me that he'd find a way to help me get out. Little did I know that we both had the same plans."

"I'm glad we could help you."

She grinned. "Me too," she said with a shy smile that he found to be adorable. His mother would love her. *Whoa! Where the fuck had that thought come from? Your heart, you idiot. Did the blast do that much damage to your brain? You like this girl. You care for her. You're attracted to her. What in the hell are you waiting for?* He wanted to flick the little devil off his shoulder.

"So, next Saturday—Frost and Autumn's baby shower. What kind of baby shower is it exactly? She asked.

"It's a couples thing," he replied, and her eyes widened. He then realized what he said. "Shit. Not a couples only type of thing. But one where both men and women are invited."

She started to laugh. "I understand. I know what a *couples' baby shower* is."

He breathed a sigh of relief. "Does that mean you'll go?"

"How about you let me get through the dinner on Saturday night, and then I'll start penciling in dates on my calendar." She joked.

"Smartass."

She stuck her tongue out at him, and he laughed.

"Where are they registered?"

"Where are who registered?" He asked and giggled.

"The parents silly—Frost and Autumn. Most people having a baby or adopting register somewhere so people can pick out a gift."

He ran his hand over his head. "Shit, I don't know."

She held up her hand. "Don't worry about it. I'll take care of the gift."

CHAPTER TWELVE

Diego kept a close eye on Campbell as he and the rest of the guys sat out on the back deck having drinks and appetizers that Campbell had prepared.

He had been a little worried earlier when she had started to freak out. Once he talked with her and calmed her down, he realized it was just nerves. And it was understandable. She didn't know everyone and probably felt like an outsider. But he was confident that she would open up and fit right in with the others with her personality.

"Damn, man. Campbell knows how to cook." Dino admitted as he took a corn chip, scooped up another helping of buffalo chicken dip, and popped it into his mouth. "I've had many versions of this dip, but I have to say, this is by far the best."

"What's for dinner anyway?" Potter asked as he kept an eye on his oldest daughter Alejandra, who played in the yard with Cody, Frost's son, Sienna, Irish's daughter, and the three dogs, Zuma, Nigel, and Beretta. They had a house full.

Diego laughed as Nigel, the giant Great Dane, barreled over Sienna. She got up laughing and brushed herself off.

"Umm...I think she made a roast, with potatoes and vegetables, along with a salad and bread. She also said she had a whole different menu for the kids if they didn't like what we were having. She's been in the kitchen the whole day, so there could be more."

"She seems to be getting along with the others," Frost said.

"Has she opened up any more about her past?" Stitch asked, and Diego knew where he was going with that question. That stemmed from the wounds on her arms when Stitch came over and helped.

Diego didn't want to divulge too many details without first speaking to Campbell. He knew it had taken a lot for her to open up the other night and tell him what she endured living with that asshole.

"She and I talked a bit the other day after you guys left." He played with the paper label on his bottle. "Let's just say she's been through a lot of both verbal and physical abuse, not to mention the strain on her mentally from losing her parents. I did find out she has a sister."

"Really?" Ace stated as if he was shocked by that revelation.

Diego nodded, then told them a little about Lizzy's story.

"That's a damn shame. Campbell doesn't have any idea where she could be?" Skittles asked.

"Nope."

"When we were talking with Fred, he mentioned she used to dance until she was involved in some accident. Did she get that limp from the accident?" Irish asked.

Diego bit the inside of his cheek as the anger started to boil inside him as he recalled Campbell telling him how that fucker had taken a baseball bat to her leg.

He looked at Irish with fire in his eyes. "It wasn't an accident. And yes, she was left with the limp as the result of it."

At that moment, they could hear loud laughter from inside, and when Diego glanced through the open door, he smiled as he watched Campbell came out of her shell.

Campbell thought sitting around and being the new person would be awkward, but she had been primarily mistaken. She couldn't have asked to be anywhere else as she sat in the living room with Alex, Tenley, Autumn, Bailey, Mia, Arianna, and Anna Grace. They were all different in their own unique ways, but at the same time, were alike. They were all effortless to talk to, and had surprised the hell out of her when they had given her a hug when they were introduced. Their kindness literally brought tears to her eyes.

She felt kind of silly that she got herself worked up over nothing. Earlier, before everyone started to arrive, her nerves had gotten the best of her and almost sent her into a full-on panic attack. But now, as she sat on the couch in between Alex and Bailey, she was cool as a cucumber. They were just killing time while dinner finished up in the oven.

Tenley, Potter's wife, got up and walked over to the pack-n-play set up in the corner of the living room and laid one of her babies down for a nap. Campbell thought she said her name was Kensi. Her twin sister Kelsey was fast asleep in Arianna's arms. They were so cute.

"So Campbell, Diego told us that it was you who did most of the work in his office and the bedrooms upstairs. Is that really true?" Tenley asked as she sat back down on the other couch.

Campbell grinned and nodded. "It is. As I told Diego, he was at the base the first two days after I got here, and I had no idea what to do. I don't like to sit around and do nothing. So, I saw an opportunity to help him out."

"Well, that was very sweet of you, not to mention you did a fantastic job. Diego's office looks amazing. And I can't wait until you guys get the furniture in for the rooms upstairs," Alex said with excitement.

"I can't either, especially the room with the big windows for all that natural light to come through. And then paired with the yellow accent furnishings that Diego and I picked out, it'll bring the entire room together."

Right as she ended her sentence, she realized something. Would she even be around when all those things came in? Would her ordeal with Mitchell be over, and she'd be free to leave? Did she want to go? A sad feeling began to overcome her. How could she feel this attached after only being in Diego's house for little over a week? Those were all questions that she needed to think about and find answers to.

She hadn't realized she had zoned out in front of everyone until Alex gently touched her arm.

"Campbell? Are you okay?" Alex asked her.

Campbell shook the cobwebs from inside her head and offered Alex a small smile. "Sorry. I tend to zone out every now and then."

Alex reciprocated the smile. "Don't be sorry. It happens to all of us."

Campbell felt a little embarrassed being caught stuck in her thoughts. She stood up.

"Let me go check on dinner. It should be ready. Do any of you need another drink or anything else?"

Anna Grace smiled. "I think we're all good."

"Do you need any help getting anything ready?" Autumn asked from the recliner where she had her feet elevated. The poor woman was eight months pregnant and looked it too.

Bailey chuckled. "Yeah, good luck if Frost catches you on your feet."

Autumn rolled her eyes. "He's been a pain in my ass these last few weeks. I'm surprised he lets me wipe myself."

Alex snorted a laugh. "Hey, he just cares about you and that little bun you've got in the oven."

Autumn sighed. "I know he means well. I'm just frustrated that I can't do some things on my own."

"To keep your sanity, just let it go and accept whatever help he offers even though it drives you crazy. Potter was the same way when I was pregnant with the twins."

"Maybe," Autumn replied on a sigh.

"Well, you don't have much longer to go," Arianna said.

"Yes, our little family is expanding," Mia stated as she covered her belly with her hand, and Campbell wondered if Mia was expecting as well. She waited to see if someone said something, but she excused herself to check on the food when no one did.

Once Campbell was out of earshot, Alex turned to the other ladies and grinned.

"I like her a lot," she said, referring to Campbell.

"Me too," Tenley seconded, followed by the others all agreeing.

"She's a little timid and withdrawn. I don't know what her backstory is because the guys won't say, but you can see in her eyes there's some sadness in her." Alex said.

"I'm sure she has a story, just like all of us did at one time." Arianna followed up with.

Autumn smiled. "And when she's ready, she'll tell her story."

Diego had just stood up to check on Campbell to see if she needed any help in getting dinner set when Alejandra climbed the stairs to the deck and jumped in Potter's lap. To this day, he'd never forget when Potter and the team met the little girl. They had all been in Ecuador trying to find Tenley when she went missing while working with a humanitarian organization after a massive earthquake struck the South American country. Sadly, Alejandra's parents hadn't survived the disaster. Tenley had been taking care of the little girl, but when she managed to steal Potter's heart in a matter of seconds, he and Tenley ended up adopting her.

Alejandra put her arms around Potter's neck and gave him a big hug, and Diego grinned. He'd never thought he'd see the day when Potter gave his heart to a woman, let alone a child. It was truly heartwarming to watch.

"What was that for?" Potter asked her, and she gave him a cheeky grin.

"You looked like you needed a hug, daddy," Alejandra giggled. Potter smirked, then kissed her on the head.

She reached for the bowl of chips and grabbed a handful before she looked at Irish.

"Sienna said you were getting her a pink rabbit. Is that true?"

Looking confused with his eyebrows furrowed, Irish looked at Alejandra.

"A pink rabbit?"

"Dude, you can't have a rabbit with a cat," Skittles said, and Diego agreed. Although if he had to choose between a rabbit and Sienna's cat Mr. Whiskers, he'd have to go with the rabbit. He'd never tell Sienna that her cat was fucking weird, not to mention he had no personality and hated everyone.

"I'm not getting her a rabbit. I don't know where she got that idea from."

Alejandra just shrugged her shoulders as if she didn't care either way, then leaped off Potter's lap and went back down to the yard with other kids.

Suddenly, Irish blurted out, "Oh shit!"

When Diego looked at his friend and teammate, his face was redder than a shiny new fire engine.

Ace chuckled. "By the look on your face, Irish, I'm guessing there's a really good story behind the rabbit."

Irish picked his beer up and guzzled about half of the bottle before he set it back down.

"If any of you tell Bailey I told you this, I swear I'll find a way to make your lives a living hell." When everyone agreed, though they were all grinning, Irish continued. "So, the other night, Bailey and I were fooling around with her favorite toy." Potter choked on a laugh as if knowing where the story was heading. "Just as she was about to hit her limit, the damn thing died. She was pissed and started carrying on about needing to buy a new rabbit. Around that time, I heard something outside our bedroom door. When I went to check, I found Sienna coming out of the hall bathroom."

Ace started laughing. "So, your daughter overheard you and Bailey in the heat of passion discussing rabbit vibrators, and your curious six-year-old mistook your words and now thinks you guys are buying her a pink bunny rabbit?"

Diego chuckled. "That's classic."

Irish ran his fingers through his blonde hair. "I don't know what to do."

"You need to tell Bailey," Stitch said, trying to keep a straight face. It was all too funny. Poor Irish, the one man on the team who none of them thought would ever settle down, had his hands full with his niece turned daughter. But for the rest of them, it provided great entertainment.

Campbell plated all the food and set the serving dishes on the dining room table. Diego had brought in another table and connected it to the big table to accommodate everyone. She looked around the room and smiled. Everything was in its place and looked perfect.

She called out to everyone and told them that dinner was ready. While everyone settled, she headed back into the kitchen to wash the dirty pots and pans and wipe down the countertops.

She opened the refrigerator to put away the large butter container when she saw the two bottles of white wine she had set in there to chill so it could be served with dinner. She grabbed them, and as she walked into the dining room with the wine in her hands, she stopped in her tracks when she was met by the fifteen pairs of eyes staring at her. They hadn't even started to eat. In fact, the food was untouched and still where she had placed it on the table. Diego was already out of his chair, walking toward her with a concerned expression.

Her stomach suddenly got a huge knot in it. Maybe they didn't like the food. Or perhaps the centerpiece full of the spring flowers she chose wasn't good enough. An uneasy feeling surrounded her, and she felt like she was going to be sick. She went to turn around, but Diego gently reached for her elbow, stopping her. He looked down at her, and his expression softened.

"Is everything okay?" He asked as he slid his hands down her arms.

He was asking her if everything was okay. Shouldn't she be the one asking him that?

"Why isn't anyone eating?" She asked in a whispered voice, but she knew the others most likely heard because the room was utterly silent.

He smiled. "We're waiting for you."

Surprised but confused, she took a step back and looked around him. They were all still looking in her direction. She looked back at Diego.

"Why?"

"What do you mean why? It isn't polite to start eating until everyone is seated at the table."

"But I'm the hostess, and everything is going to get cold."

"Well then, I guess *we* better sit so *we* can eat." He pressed his hand to the small of her back, giving her a little nudge. He pulled out her chair and motioned for her to sit. Once she was seated, he took the chair next to her. She looked up, and again she seemed to be the main attraction. This time she received warm smiles from everyone before they all started passing the food around.

She sat there for a few seconds watching everyone. She felt a little off-kilter because Mitchell would never have allowed her to eat with everyone. She felt a hand on her knee, and when she turned her head, Diego was watching her.

"You good?" He asked.

She offered him a faint smile and nodded her head.

He leaned forward and surprised her when he kissed her cheek.

"Thank you. Everything looks delicious," he whispered softly in her ear, and again she felt those butterflies fluttering in her belly.

He gave her knee one more squeeze then released it so he could place some food on his plate. When Campbell looked across the table, Alex gave her a big smile then winked, and Campbell couldn't help but smile back.

After dinner and everyone complimenting Campbell's cooking, they all worked as a team to clear the table, which seemed foreign to Campbell. Where she came from, no man would touch a dirty dish, much less clean it. She had to admit it was funny watching the guys do the dishes. They were so structured in everything they did. They had an assembly line in place. One person scraped the food from the plates; the next would scrub it before passing it on to the next person to be rinsed, before being handed to the others to be dried and put away.

Campbell stood off to the side with the other ladies watching their men look all domesticated.

"Campbell, where did you learn to entertain and cook? Everything was spot on, and no detail went unnoticed." Arianna asked her.

"Where I lived before, we entertained a lot. I was always the hostess. Most of the time, it's something I enjoy doing. It's fun to create a theme then design and plan around it. Even if it's just dinner."

"If you don't mind me asking, why did you hesitate when coming to sit down at the table?" Anna Grace asked.

Campbell twisted her fingers together nervously, and Alex must have noticed her nervousness.

"Sweetie, you don't have to tell us if it makes you uncomfortable."

She wasn't sure what the other guys might have told them.

"Umm...I wasn't allowed to sit with the guests we were entertaining unless I was permitted to."

"Seriously?"

"Afraid so."

"You were in a bad place," Alex said as a statement, not a question.

She looked around at the women who stood with her and had welcomed her with open arms into their little circle of friendship. She didn't know what had overcome her, but she found herself wanting to tell her story just as she did with Diego a few nights before. She pulled them all out on the back deck while the guys finished up in the kitchen and proceeded to open her heart a little more. She told them about losing her parents, her sister, then everything she had been through with Mitchell, including the altercation that left her with the limp.

"I'm so sorry you had to endure that abuse," Alex told her before she gave her a big hug. And boy, had Campbell needed that hug. Laying everything out on the table was mentally exhausting.

Bailey stepped up next and hugged her. "Just so you know, you aren't alone. Each one of us has our past that we've overcome."

"Always remember that the life in front of you is more important than the one behind you," Autumn told her before hugging her.

"You'll learn quickly that us girls stick together," Tenley said and hugged her.

"And, when one of us is down, another is there to pick us up." Arianna followed up on Tenley's comment. She, too, hugged Campbell.

"We're not just friends; we're family," Mia said, also hugging Campbell.

Anna Grace was the last one to step forward. "I think what we're all trying to say is welcome to our family." Everyone laughed and agreed. Campbell shocked herself when she hugged Anna Grace. She felt the tears build in her eyes but blinked rapidly to dispel them.

Before long, the guys made their appearance.

"What are you ladies conjuring up over here?" Ace asked as he hugged Alex from behind. It was a public show of affection, and Campbell wished one day she'd have someone who touched and looked at her the way these badass men looked at their women. She ignored the sudden pang of jealousy. It wasn't the time nor the place for her inner green monster to come out. Then as if Diego was reading her mind, he walked up and placed his hands on her hips. And holy hell, she almost came out of her skin from the feeling of his gentle yet possessive touch.

"Well, are you all going to answer Ace, or are you planning some top-secret mission?"

Tenley snorted. "Yeah, like anything is a secret around you guys. I swear all of you have some sort of radar or homing device that alerts you when any of us have a thought." She blurted out, and everyone laughed. Even Campbell caught herself smiling, and for the first time in years, she felt as if she finally belonged.

CHAPTER THIRTEEN

Mitchell sat listening to a friend of his who worked for the Division of Mining and Reclamation. Not only was he dealing with Campbell's unruly behavior and disappearance, but he was also in the midst of doing damage control to save the sale of his mine.

"I've managed to get most damaging evidence removed from the file before it heads to the review board," Gary told him.

"Did you get the updated logs that Vinny sent over?"

"I did, and I've had them added to the case file."

Mitchell sat back in the leather chair. He was on a private jet that Igor had chartered for him for his return trip to the states.

"Good. With the current file where it stands now, am I looking at any criminal charges?"

"No. No criminal charges, but I also didn't want to make it look perfect either, so I tweaked a few things, and you'll most likely have to pay a fine mainly for issues surrounding the equipment maintenance."

"I can handle that."

"Have you been able to trace who submitted the complaint and documents?"

"No. All the documents were submitted anonymously via the mail. But whoever did it must've had access to the mine's logs and administrative records."

Mitchell thought about that. Many of the supervisors and upper-level management would have access to the logs, but only a handful of people had access to administrative records. He'd have to do some investigating when he got home.

"So, if no criminal charges are pending, and the minor issues that were brought forward in the complaint are corrected, and I pay the fine, am I good to close on the sale of the mine?"

"I don't see why you couldn't. As long as everything has been corrected and passes the inspections."

"Alright then. I appreciate your hastiness in getting this taken care of for me. If anything changes, you know where to find me."

Before Gary could speak, Mitchell disconnected the line. He leaned his head back and started to think. Who would have gone behind his back and tried to ruin him? Anyone who had ever dared to blow the whistle on any illegal doings at the mine had been dealt with and were no longer a threat unless they had help and weren't acting alone.

He picked up the phone and dialed Vinny.

"Hello?"

"Get a list of every employee who has ever threatened or attempted to file a complaint against the mine."

"What's going on?"

"We have a snitch to smoke out."

"Sounds interesting. I'll have everything for when you get here."

"Great. Any word on the other situation we're dealing with?"

"No. Not a word and nobody has seen her."

Mitchell took a deep breath and looked out the window of the plane. The sky around him looked dark and dreary, just like his current mood.

"Somebody knows where she is. She had to have had help. Belle couldn't have stayed hidden this long all on her own."

"But who? We've gone back to that diner she worked at, and they still claim they haven't seen her or spoken to her. And just to be sure, I even had Allen stake the place out and follow the owners home. There's no sign of her being in town."

Mitchell gritted his teeth. He didn't need this from her right now. Everything was falling into place. He only needed a few more weeks, and he and Belle would've been saying goodbye to the mountains of West Virginia and starting their lives in their new home of Siberia.

Suddenly, an idea came to him. It was a long shot, but it was all he had right now.

"You said she left her cell phone, right?"

"Yeah. It was in the car. I put it in your office."

"Do me a favor and get the phone, then look up the name Lizzy or Elizabeth and jot down the phone number associated with that name. Bring it with you when you come to the airport to pick me up."

"Will do. Who's Lizzy?"

"That could be our ticket to finding Belle."

CHAPTER FOURTEEN

Diego pulled his truck in front of the garage. He was so glad that he was able to drive again. Derek had called earlier and asked if he could come into the office because the mission they were anticipating looked like it could be happening sooner rather than later. He just hoped they wouldn't get the call until after his next doctor's appointment and hopefully his last. That was scheduled a week and a half from tomorrow.

He reached over into the back seat to grab his bag, and when he did, his stomach growled loudly, reminding him that he needed food. He was starving. He never got a chance to eat with all the meetings and phone calls, and he didn't take anything with him. He wondered and hoped that Campbell cooked up something for them. Ever since they went to the grocery store last week and stocked the pantry, freezer, and refrigerator, she had cooked dinner every night. She was also coming out of her shell and becoming more opinionated, which was great to see. She was taking charge of her life just like everyone wanted for her.

He was also finding himself becoming more and more attached to her as the days passed. People could call it whatever they wanted, but he had definitely developed strong feelings for her. There had been times when he had caught her looking at him, and he also wondered if those feelings were reciprocated.

As soon as he opened the front door to the house, he was hit by an aroma that pulled him further inside and made his mouth instantly water. He couldn't put his finger on it, but damn, did it entice him. He heard music playing and smiled when he heard one of his mom's favorite Latin songs, Pareja Del Ano, coming through the surround speakers in the house. It was a great song to dance to.

He wiped his boots on the mat and rounded the corner to the kitchen when the sight of Campbell dancing stopped him. The double doors to the refrigerator were open as she moved gracefully with rhythm to the music's up-tempo beat. The sight of her left him spellbound as she incorporated ballet into the dance mix. He quietly moved further into the space, taking in something he'd never seen in the two weeks she'd been living with him. He stared at the most beautiful, toned legs he'd ever laid eyes on, even with her scars.

Not missing a beat, she closed the doors to the refrigerator as she kept her back to him. She danced her way to the stove and stirred something in the pot while her hips continued to sway to the music. Every time she stood on her tiptoes, her leg muscles would flex, and Diego could only stand there and admire her. She was a beautiful dancer, and he couldn't understand why she had given it up. Even Fred had commented that her accident had ruined her dancing career. But from Diego's vantage point, she was far from ruined.

Before he could announce himself, she twirled around, and as soon as her eyes locked on him, she screamed and dropped the glass that was in her hand, causing it to shatter as it hit the tiled floor, sending shards of glass all over the place.

He saw the panic on her face, and she wanted to move. He looked down at all the glass and her bare feet, and he yelled at her.

"Don't move!"

She froze, and the frightened look on her face broke his heart. Dammit, he hadn't yelled at her to reprimand her. He didn't want her stepping on the broken glass and cutting herself. Within seconds he saw her eyes start to glisten.

"Dammit Campbell, I'm sorry."

He quickly moved around the center island, the glass crunching under his boots with every step he took. Once he got to her, he lifted her up and set her on the counter. He placed his hands on each side of her on the counter. He stepped closer; the movement made her part her legs to make room for his body.

She continued to stare at him, and he used his thumb to dab her cheeks where a few tears had spilled over. Then out of nowhere, she started rambling.

"I'm so sorry. I was trying to surprise you with dinner. I didn't hear you come in. Please don't be mad at me for breaking your glass. I swear I'll buy a new one. Well, when I find a job and start making some money. I'll even buy you a new set. Just let me down, so I can clean up my mess."

Diego couldn't take it anymore, and he started laughing. She was too damn adorable when she got flustered.

She scrunched her nose up at him. "Are you laughing at me?"

"No, Campbell, not at you directly. I'm laughing at the situation, although I have to say you are damn cute when you ramble."

Her cheeks turned red, and she lowered her head. He placed his finger under her chin, and she lifted her head.

"Don't be embarrassed and thank you for making dinner. It was really nice of you." He tapped her nose. "Now stay put until I get the broom and sweep the glass up."

Once all the glass was swept up and, in the trash, he came back over to the counter. She was still sitting there watching him.

"So, what's for dinner? Because I have to say it smells delicious, and I'm starving."

She shrugged her shoulders. "It isn't much. I wasn't sure when you were getting home, so I made chili and hot dogs for chili dogs, and I cut up some potatoes to make French fries. Do you like cheese on your fries?"

He smiled. "That actually sounds really good, and yes, I love cheese fries."

He gripped her hips and helped her off the counter. He didn't release her right away, and she placed her hands on his forearms. She still looked a little unsure.

"You good?"

"Yeah, but are you sure you're not mad about the glass? I'll understand if you want to punish me."

What the fuck did she mean by punishing her? He wanted to ask her so many questions right now. Did the guy she lived with punish her whenever she would make mistakes or have an accident? He grew angry thinking that.

"Campbell, I want you to listen to me very carefully. I will never lay a hand on you out of anger. Nor will I allow any man to touch you inappropriately. It was just a glass. I was more worried about you getting hurt." He wasn't sure what made him do it, but he leaned down and kissed her forehead before taking her hand and leading her to the table. He pulled out a chair for her, and she sat.

"Since you cooked, I'll get the food and then clean up afterward."

He turned, but then she reached out and grabbed his hand. "Thank you, Diego."

"Anytime, sweetheart. Now let's eat, and then if you're feeling up to it, we can watch a movie together."

After dinner, Diego went to his room to take a quick shower. Now, as they sat on the couch watching NetFlix, he couldn't stop his eyes from wandering over to her. She looked so content curled up under a blanket with a pillow on her lap that she would use to shield her eyes when a suspenseful part came in the show, which he thought was funny. But there was one thing he couldn't shake from his mind. He wanted to press her more about what she meant about being punished. He was well aware that Mitchell was abusive, but what had he done to her in the form of punishment?

He waited until the movie was over when she started to sit up and pushed the blanket off her. His eyes went to her legs, and immediately he regretted it when she tried to put the blanket back in place, but he stopped her.

"Don't." He told her softly. He didn't want her to be ashamed of her past injury.

"I don't like people seeing what he did to me."

"I get it, but you can't go around in life hiding who you are because someone did something out of your control." He leaned forward and cupped her cheek. "Whether you realize it or not, you're a smart and beautiful woman. Embrace your features, and be proud of who you are and what you represent."

"What do I represent?"

"You are a survivor. I won't lie, you've been through hell and back, but you decided to take your life back."

"I guess I never thought about it that way. I'm just mad at myself that I let it go as far as it did, and I paid the price for it." She motioned to her leg.

He swallowed hard. "Earlier, when you dropped the glass, you mentioned punishments. What else did he do to you?"

Her eyes got wider. He surprised her with that question, but it was a question that weighed heavily on him, and he couldn't let it go. She sat there for a minute or two and didn't say anything. But then she turned toward him.

"There were times where if I didn't do something correctly, Mitchell would punish me."

When she didn't elaborate, he raised his eyebrow as if telling her to continue.

She took a deep breath before she twisted her wrist and showed him the underside. He saw two circular scars that resembled burns, and his stomach instantly felt uneasy.

"He put those there when I didn't clean his cigar ashtray out," she calmly told him.

Diego thought his head was going to fucking explode. The asshole had fucking burned her. Then he got angrier when she tried to make a joke about it by saying, "I only made that mistake twice."

"Campbell, that's not okay," he reprimanded, but she snapped back at him.

"I know it's not, but there's not much I can do when the person assaulting me is much more powerful and holds my life in his hands."

Diego ran his hands down his face. He got it—he understood, but he didn't like it. It set his stomach on fire, knowing the shit she endured at the hands of an abuser.

"Is that the only time he *punished* you?"

She shook her head. "No, and I'm not sure I want to tell you anymore because you're already mad at me."

He shook his head. "No. There's a difference. Am I mad? Damn, right I am. But am I mad at you? Hell no. I'm mad at the fucker who treated you like that. For someone who says he loves you, he sure has a sick way of showing it."

"Just for the record. I never loved him."

"You didn't?"

"No, although he forced me to tell him that I did. But I didn't mean it."

"I'm sorry," he told her, and she turned and gave him a funny look.

"Why are you sorry? You haven't done anything to be sorry for. In fact, I'm the one who should be saying sorry. Here, you've had to readjust your life because of me."

He realized the conversation was getting out of control. The last thing he wanted her to think was that she was an inconvenience, because she was far from that. Her personality, kindness, and unselfishness had opened his heart.

"Campbell, I haven't had to readjust my life. This is normal. This is what we do for a living. We help people get out of all different kinds of situations, amongst other things." Things she wouldn't want to know.

"So, I'm a job?"

Shit. He was screwing this up. "No! I don't consider you a job. And to be honest, I thought I liked living alone, but since you've been here, I've enjoyed the company."

He saw a spark in her eyes when he said that.

"I guess we both are thankful then."

He grinned. "I guess so."

Slowly her smile faded and was replaced with a look of gloom.

Diego turned to her, his smile fading away. "The fear and sadness on your face right now is destroying me. Tell me what just went through your mind."

"If Mitchell finds me, he'll make me pay the ultimate price for what I've done."

All feelings set aside, Diego reached over and pulled her into his arms and hugged her tight. He smiled when he felt her arms slide around his shoulders.

"I won't let him, Campbell. I promise you're safe with me."

"Thank you," she whispered.

As he stared over her shoulder, he noticed a pile of wrapped gifts sitting in the corner. He eased back from their embrace. He saw she wiped her eye.

"What are those?" He asked and nodded toward the presents.

Her eyes popped open wide, and her cheeks pinkened. "Oh! I sort of got carried away while buying a gift for Frost and Autumn's baby shower."

There had to have been eight or nine gifts stacked up.

"Did you buy everything on their registry?" He teased, and she smiled.

"No, but it was hard to choose just one thing. Shopping for baby items can be addicting. Everything is so darn cute, and you just want to buy it all. But in my defense, I at least stuck with a theme and bought all the bath items they wanted; the tub, towels, washcloths, bath toys, and things like that."

He loved her enthusiasm and was glad that she decided to go to the baby shower.

"Okay. What do I owe you?"

She shook her head. "Absolutely nothing. You and your friends have done so much already. Let me get this. I already signed the card from both of us."

This was one battle he wasn't going to fight, so he conceded. "Alright. But I insist on taking you out to dinner one night."

She smiled. "Deal."

CHAPTER FIFTEEN

Campbell walked into Bayside with Diego. She was a little skeptical about the place when they first pulled into the parking lot. In all honesty, it looked like a dump from the outside. Diego had read her expression because he informed her that Paul, the owner, kept it that way to keep tourists away. At first, she didn't understand why a business owner would want to keep customers from coming in, but Diego then explained it was because a lot of military personnel from the bases in the area came there due to there being no tourists. It was a place for them to unwind and not be bothered. She hadn't been aware of the following that the SEALs had, especially the women.

They were both carrying gifts for the new parents. They walked over to the table that held the other gifts and put them down.

Diego chuckled. "At least we weren't the only ones to splurge."

Campbell smiled as she looked at the many stacks of the gifts already on the table. "Welcoming a new baby is special." She told him and grinned.

"Yes, they are."

She locked gazes with him. She loved his dark brown eyes, paired with his sexy smirk. Alex's voice broke the invisible pull between them.

"Campbell!"

When Campbell turned, Alex was smiling and waving her over. "Come join us."

She looked at Diego, and he winked. "Go on. I'm gonna go talk to the guys."

She walked over to the table where all the ladies were sitting. She was still a bit nervous.

Mia pulled a chair out. "Have a seat next to me."

"Isn't that Stitch's seat?"

She waved her hand in the air. "It's fine. The guys will be over there for a while catching up with their friends."

Campbell eyed the eight other men who were talking with Diego and the others at a nearby table.

Alex leaned over. "That's Bravo Team. They're SEALs as well. The guy with dirty blonde hair and grey eyes sitting across from Ace is Bear. He's the team leader. Then going around the table from right to left is Joker, Duke, Playboy, Aussie, Nails, Snow, and Jay Bird. You'll see them around here often. If we get a chance, I'll introduce you to them."

Campbell couldn't stop staring. They were huge.

"Goodness, what does the military feed these guys?"

Alex snickered. "They are, but I can assure you that any of them would have your back in a heartbeat."

Campbell looked at Alex. "Maybe you guys, but not me."

"Why is that?"

"Because this is just a temporary home for me."

Alex glanced over Campbell's shoulder and grinned. Curious about what she was smiling at, Campbell stole a peek and met Diego's chocolate eyes.

"I think you might want to start thinking about permanent residency," Alex said with a chuckle.

Campbell swung her head around and looked at Alex.

"Why would you say that?"

Alex gave her a soft smile. "Honey, I recognize that look on Diego's face."

"What look would that be?"

"It's the same look I caught Ace giving me, that Potter gave Tenley, that Frost gave Autumn…shall I continue down the list of guys?"

Campbell held her hand up. "No. I get the point."

She glanced over her shoulder again in Diego's direction. Could Alex be right? Would he want her to stay?

"You didn't tell us he took a fucking baseball bat to her leg," Frost stated.

"Or, a damn belt to her arms." Ace followed. They were both angry but made sure they kept their voices down so Campbell wouldn't hear them.

Diego looked at the others, who appeared just as pissed as Frost and Ace were. The question was how they found out, because he never told them. He looked at Stitch first because Stitch knew about her arms.

Stitch held his hands up. "Don't look at me. I never said a word."

Frost turned on Stitch. "You knew about it?"

"I only found out about her arms the other day."

"I asked him to come over when I caught Campbell trying to hide the injury from me. They were really red still, and I was afraid of an infection setting in."

"How did you guys find out?" Diego asked, glancing at the table where Campbell was sitting, seeming to be enjoying herself.

"Autumn told me. She said that Campbell told her and the others at your house last weekend."

"Yeah, Alex asked me if I knew." Ace said.

Diego took a drink from his bottle and set it down.

"Campbell told me about it last week. I wasn't keeping it intentionally from you guys. It just wasn't my story to tell. I never lied to you. Her limp had come from that so-called accident, which you all are now fully aware wasn't an accident at all."

Bear looked at Diego. "Why did she cover for the asshole?"

"Fear," Diego admitted. It was what Campbell had told him. "Fear of what he'd do to her next. He's untouchable in the town he lives in. He's the perfect example of how money talks."

"That's fucked up," Joker, one of Bear's teammates, said before storming off toward the bar. Diego noticed that Joker was full of piss and vinegar, and he wondered what had happened to set him off.

"Don't mind him," Bear said as he kept an eye on Joker. "Something's had him riled up for the last couple of days."

"So, how long is she staying?" Duke asked. He was a medic for the Bravo Team.

That was a question Diego couldn't answer. If he had a choice, he wouldn't want her to leave.

"As long as it takes to ensure her safety, or if she wants to." He noticed the smirks on Ace and Irish's faces and knew what they were thinking. Hell, if he was an honest man, which he was, he had the same thoughts. He didn't want her to leave. They had fallen into a routine together, and if she left, he'd feel as if a part of him left with her—his heart."

Campbell had excused herself to use the restroom, and on her way back to the table, she noticed off to the right of the hallway, there was a decent-sized room that sat empty and dark. She stopped to look at it. With the light from the outside coming through the large glass sliding doors, she could get a view of what the room offered. In her opinion, it seemed as if the space went unused and became a place to store items, such as the stacks of chairs, piles of tablecloths, along with many other furnishings.

Immediately, her mind went into her creative mode of what she could do with the room to utilize it for profit. It was the perfect size to rent for private parties, and with access to the patio deck, they'd be able to fit more people.

"Hey, there you are. We thought you got lost." Arianna said from the doorway.

Campbell turned and smiled. "Sorry, this room caught my attention."

Arianna wrinkled her forehead. "What's so special about this room?"

"Why don't you guys use it?"

Arianna shrugged her shoulders. "That's a good question. I honestly don't know. Years ago, it was used for poker nights, but I'm not sure what happened. I wasn't home much during that time."

Campbell remembered Diego telling her that Arianna had previously worked for the FBI and had done a jaunt uncover. But after a falling out with the Bureau and almost being killed, she resigned and now splits her time between helping her dad run Bayside and working as a Forensics Accountant for Tink's security company.

Campbell twirled around, getting another look at the space.

"You should think about fixing it up and using it to rent space for parties. You'd make a killing, especially in the warmer months when you can open those sliders, and guests could utilize both the patio deck and the room. Shoot, I'd rent it just for the view itself."

Arianna looked around. "Hmm...I never thought about it, but you might be onto something. I'll have to look into it."

"I think the food was just brought out if you're hungry," Arianna said, and Campbell grinned.

"I'm actually starving. I think for the first time since I arrived in town, I slept in. Then I was helping Diego with things around the house, and we both lost track of time and never ate anything."

Arianna grinned mischievously. "You and Diego seem to be getting along really well."

Campbell blushed, and Arianna snickered.

"Hey, don't be embarrassed. Diego's a great guy. I can tell he cares for you. You've got my vote, along with everyone else out there," Arianna told her, then winked.

As everyone sat around the large table eating and talking, Campbell found herself deep in conversation with the kids. She listened to them talk about what they were doing in school since the school year was ending. Sienna was finishing Kindergarten, Alejandra was in second, while Cody was in fifth. All three of them were well mannered, polite, not to mention full of personality—especially Sienna. That little girl was a firecracker. Diego had shared some stories about the little dynamo that had Campbell in stitches laughing. Mainly the story of when she served the team canned cat food instead of tuna fish.

"So, I heard you guys are having career day in your school this week. Have you had any interesting guest speakers?"

Cody spoke first. Campbell already admired the boy for his heroic actions when he saved his mom last year from some psycho who had kidnapped her.

"We had a Cyber Warfare Operations Officer come and speak to our class the other day. It was pretty cool hearing about what they do in developing programs to protect infrastructure, and how they support communication operations all over the world."

"That does sound cool. Is that what you're interested in?"

Cody grinned and shook his head before looking over at Frost. "No. I'm planning on following in my dad's footsteps and making the SEALs."

Campbell smiled as she admired the bond between the father and son. She had learned from Diego that Cody's biological dad and Autumn's first husband was a Marine who was killed in action a few years ago in Iraq. But watching the interaction between the two, Frost treated Cody as if he were his own flesh and blood.

Campbell looked at Alejandra. She was a beautiful girl with her dark olive complexion and curly jet-black hair. In a few years, she was going to have the boys beating down her door. Although having a dad like Potter, the boys may rethink their actions.

"What do you want to be when you grow up?" Campbell asked her.

With her nose scrunched up, she answered, "I don't know. I love animals, so maybe a veterinarian like Aunt Mia. But I also want to help people like my mommy does. So maybe a nurse."

Campbell smiled. "Well, they're both wonderful choices."

She looked at Sienna, who sat between Irish and Bailey eating a cheeseburger that was so big Campbell didn't think she could even finish it.

"What about you, Sienna? What do you want to be when you grow up?"

The blonde hair, blue-eyed cutie put her cheeseburger down and wiped her mouth just like a little lady. She smiled and looked up at Irish and Bailey as if she was so excited to tell everyone.

"Well, Katie's mommy came to our class today, and she sounds like she has a really cool job that I think I'd be really good at. And so does my teacher."

Campbell grinned. "Well, now you've piqued my curiosity."

"I want to be a prostitute!" Sienna announced loudly and proudly, and Campbell swore the entire restaurant went radio silent.

"What the fuck?" Irish uttered as he stared at his little girl as if she had grown two heads. His earlier smile had disappeared from his face.

Bailey appeared as if she wanted to say something, but no words came out every time she opened her mouth. And as funny as it sounded, and looked, nobody was laughing.

"Daddy, what's a prosti—?" Alejandra tried to ask Potter, but he was quick to cover her mouth with his hand.

Without warning, Bailey suddenly burst into a fit of giggles.

Irish reminded Campbell of the girl in the movie *The Exorcist* by the way he twisted his head around to look at his wife, who appeared about ready to fall over out of her chair because she was laughing so hard.

"What is wrong with you?" Irish asked Bailey, still traumatized that his daughter announced to the world that she wanted to work the corner. However, Campbell might have felt the same way if she had a daughter who did something similar.

"Oh, God," Bailey said, trying to catch her breath. She reached for her glass of water and took a drink before looking at everyone and telling them to calm down.

"Calm down?!" Irish said in a somewhat whispered, high-pitched voice. It actually made a couple of the guys snicker. "Bailey, she just said she wanted to be a prostitute."

Bailey waved Irish off and looked at Sienna, who had a blank expression. It was clear she had no idea what was happening.

"Sienna, Katie's mom is a prosecutor. She works in the courts." Bailey calmly explained.

Campbell saw everyone at the table release the breaths they had all been holding. And, within seconds, the entire table erupted in laughter.

Irish got up mumbling something incoherent and went to the bar, and Campbell was sure whatever he was ordering was making it a double.

Once the laughter died down, Campbell heard the ladies talking about going to a concert on a group date night.

"Ugh! I wish we could go. I was just telling Potter about it," Tenley said with a pout.

"Why can't you?" Campbell asked.

"Because normally Alex or Juliette would babysit the kids, and they're planning on going."

Campbell looked at Diego. "What about us? Do you care if the kids stay with us?"

Diego grinned. "I'm game."

She turned toward Bailey and Autumn. "If you guys want to go, we could watch Sienna and Cody as well."

"Frost and I weren't planning since I can hardly move around anymore," Autumn said but then smiled. "However, we could use a night alone."

Campbell smiled. "Of course, the new parents-to-be deserve a date night even if you don't leave the house."

"Seriously? You guys really don't mind?" Bailey asked, looking surprised and excited.

"No, not at all. It'll be fun."

Tenley looked up at Potter. Campbell knew they were probably worried about the babies.

"It'll be late by the time we get home," Tenley said.

"They can stay the night. You have the pack n plays, and Diego has enough bedrooms for the other kids. There aren't any beds yet, but he has some air mattresses they can sleep on."

Bailey laughed. "You won't need bedrooms. Those kids love to make forts. As long as you have a stockpile of sheets and blankets, you'll be good."

"I've got plenty around the house," Diego said.

"Thank you, Campbell. It's very nice and sweet of you to offer that," Tenley said.

Campbell smiled.

"It's the least I can do for you ladies. You all have been so nice and welcoming. It's like a breath of fresh air."

About an hour later, Campbell found herself out on the beach. She had taken her shoes off so the sand could squish between her toes—something she had wanted to experience all her life. The sun had started to set behind her over land, but the sky was a beautiful landscape of pinks and purples, with the white swirl of the clouds intertwined.

It was just as her mom described to her when they would talk about the beach. Before her mom's cancer diagnosis, they both talked about taking a mother-daughter trip to a beachside destination. But after the cancer was discovered, that trip got put on hold and was ultimately canceled once her cancer had spread.

She felt the tears emerge, and she didn't hold them back. She let the dam burst and allowed her tears to flow. Tilting her face up towards the sky, she let the last of the sun's rays caress her skin.

"Campbell?"

She turned and was met by Diego's concerned expression.

He rushed to her side and took her into his arms. "What's wrong? Are you okay?" He asked, looking her over.

She wiped the tears from her face and eyes. "I'm okay," she told him. "These are happy tears."

She sat down, and Diego followed. They both sat in silence as the sound of the waves crashing along the shore encircled them.

Diego shocked her when he reached over and took her hand into his and brought them both to his thigh, where he rested them.

"Are you sure you're okay?" He asked as he stayed focused on the ocean before them.

"Positive," she answered, then surprised herself when she leaned over and kissed his cheek.

He turned his head to face her, and she smiled. "Thank you."

"For what?"

"For bringing me here. You have no idea what this means to me. Believe it or not, this is the first time I've been to a beach."

"No?"

She grinned. "Honest to God." She then told him how she and her mom had planned to take a trip to the beach, but her cancer diagnosis derailed those plans.

"I'm sorry that you didn't get that opportunity to experience this with her."

"Me too. After she died, anytime I was feeling down, which was a lot, I would listen to the music of ocean sounds. It was relaxing, and it brought me to my happy place as I would imagine myself and my mom walking together along a soft sandy beach with the sounds of the ocean around us and the wind blowing in our hair."

She stared out at the water. "I know that probably sounds so silly, but it's the truth."

"No, Campbell. Not silly. In fact, it's beautiful, and I'm glad I was able to be here with you. Before we head home, what do you say we take a walk down the beach and bring your imagination to life?"

Campbell felt as if her heart would explode from Diego's words. She smiled.

"I'd like that."

CHAPTER SIXTEEN

As Diego climbed out of his truck and made his way up toward the front door, he was mentally preparing himself for the ruckus he was getting ready to walk into. He loved his bonus nieces and nephew, but sometimes they could be a handful, and a part of him thought that he and Campbell might have bitten off more than they could chew in regard to babysitting.

He opened the door, and the first thing that hit him was the aroma of food, and his stomach growled. Whatever it was smelled good. He was getting used to coming home to a homecooked meal on the table. He was also used to coming home to Campbell. In the few weeks she'd been living with him, she had finagled her way into his heart.

He had spoken to his mom earlier on the phone and told her that he'd be able to make it home for his dad's birthday party, and that he was bringing a guest with him. She asked so many questions that he finally had to cut her off.

Before leaving the base, he spoke with Derek and told him that he was taking Campbell with him on a long weekend trip to his hometown of South Padre Island, Texas. Derek thought it was a great idea, and since he was technically still on medical leave, he had the time.

He was beginning to feel anxious about his upcoming doctor's appointment. In fact, it was scheduled for the day after he and Campbell would return home. He figured that spending time with his family and Campbell would help take his mind off the big day and ease some of the worries.

He stood in the foyer and was surprised that it was somewhat quiet. They were hosting three kids and two babies for the night, so he had expected to walk into a three-ring circus. He followed the low voices and light music coming from the kitchen. He stood there in awe as he watched Campbell handle the three kids and two babies like they were her own platoon. Sienna was setting the table while Alejandra filled the glasses with juice or Kool-aide; he wasn't sure which it was. Cody was mixing the salad when he looked up and saw Diego standing there.

"Hey, Uncle Diego!"

He grinned. "How's it going?" He asked as he walked further into the kitchen. Both Sienna and Alejandra stopped what they were doing, ran over to him, and gave him a big hug. Cody greeted him with a handshake.

"Campbell's teaching us how presentation can dress up any type of meal," Cody informed him, and Diego glanced over to where Campbell stood by the stove. She looked gorgeous standing there in a pair of calf-length sweatpants and tank top. She had her hair piled on top of her head in some messy fashion, and it suited her. He almost laughed when she started to bite her lip again as if she was nervous.

He walked over and stood directly in front of her, and she tilted her head back to her shoulders so she could look up at him.

"You doing okay?" He asked, and she smiled.

"Yeah. The kids and I almost have dinner ready. I hope you're in the mood for some gourmet chicken nuggets, macaroni, and cheese—oh, and not the box kind." She grinned and laughed. "Sienna informed me that Bailey makes a killer mac-n-cheese, so I talked with her when she dropped Sienna off, and she told me how to make it. We also have a tossed salad that Cody is finishing up, and for dessert, we have a chocolate cake that Sienna and Alejandra made."

Diego smiled. "Sounds delicious. And it sounds like you've been busy." He leaned forward and kissed her cheek, then whispered in her ear. "Thank you."

When he pulled back, he saw how red her cheeks were, and he smiled.

"Do I have time to change?" He asked, and Campbell told him he had about five minutes before the chicken nuggets would be done. He told her he'd be right back. As he walked out of the room, he saw the two identical baby swings by the kitchen table that held Kensi and Kelsey. They were sleeping like angels.

Campbell's body was on fire, and it wasn't from standing in front of the hot stove and oven. Diego and his charm had that effect on her. He brought out a side of her that she didn't know existed. She wasn't one to sit around and fantasize about men, but since meeting Diego, she found herself more than once daydreaming about her number one when nobody was around. Hell, she could still feel his lips pressed against her cheek. She could only imagine what his lips would feel like against her—.

"Salad is done," Cody called out, making her erotic thoughts vanish into thin air.

Gathering herself, she turned around and smiled.

"Perfect. You can go ahead and put it on the table. Would you also grab the Italian dressing out of the refrigerator, please?"

While Cody did that and helped Alejandra carry the drinks over to the table, she pulled open the oven and removed the two trays of chicken nuggets. She arranged the nuggets on a platter as if she was hosting one of her parties. She opened a couple of different dipping sauces and placed them in the center of the nuggets. Next, she scooped the creamy and cheesy macaroni from its pot and put it into a bowl.

She went to turn with the bowl in her hands and nearly collided with Diego.

"Whoa!" He said and quickly took the bowl from her hands.

She looked up at him. "I'm so sorry. I didn't hear you come back in."

He grinned, and then Cody said, "Don't feel bad; they all do that. Frost has been teaching me how to walk quietly. It drives my mom crazy."

She looked back at Diego, and he smirked and lifted his one shoulder. "It's an acquired trait."

"I can see that." She replied before turning and picking up the platter of nuggets, following Diego over to the table. Alejandra and Sienna were already seated. Before she took her seat, she checked on the twins to make sure they were still sleeping, which they were. God, she could just eat them up. They were so cute.

~

Later that evening, after dinner, Diego didn't want to draw attention to himself nor admit that his head was bothering him a little. It was just a dull headache, and honestly, he couldn't tell if it was a lingering effect from his concussion, or just a tension headache. He hoped it was the latter and nothing that some over-the-counter meds couldn't take care of, which he took right before dinner.

Campbell had told him that she'd handle the cleanup and for him to help the kids build their fort in the living room. He felt bad because she had done pretty much everything from watching and entertaining the kids to preparing and cooking dinner. He had tried to argue with her, but he conceded and retreated to the living room with the kids and babies when she threatened to hit him over the head with a frying pan if he didn't go sit down.

He had helped the older kids construct a massive fort that took up over half of the living room. Sienna, Cody, and Alejandra were settled inside, watching a movie.

Diego walked over to his recliner, sunk into it, and pulled the side lever extending the footrest. Just as he got comfortable and closed his eyes, he heard a little grunt coming from one of the babies' swings. He then remembered Campbell telling him that they would probably wake within the next half hour to eat.

He waited to see if he'd hear them again. He loved the twins, but he didn't know anything about babies. His sisters had kids, but he wasn't around when they were babies, so he missed out on the feedings and diaper-changing stages of their lives. *Shucks!*

He heard the little whimper again, and soon it doubled. Potter wasn't lying when he said that when one of them did anything, the other one somehow knew and followed.

He was getting ready to get up when Campbell appeared with two bottles. She set the bottles down on the table next to his chair, then reached down into the first swing and picked up Kensi. He only knew that because the swing had her name on it. Campbell looked at Diego.

"I'm almost finished in the kitchen; do you mind feeding them their bottles? You can stay where you are."

She really didn't give him any choice as she placed Kensi in his left arm, then reached down and picked up her sister, Kelsey, and put her in his right arm. She walked over to the sofa, picked up two throw pillows, and shoved them under his arms, which helped prop the babies up. She then grabbed the bottles and gave the first one to Kensi, positioning it where Diego could grip with his fingers. Then she repeated that with Kelsey. When she stood up, she looked him over.

"You good?"

He didn't know what to say, so he just nodded his head, and she left the room and headed back into the kitchen.

He looked down at the twins as they slurped on their bottles. Kelsey was like a little piglet as she guzzled down the milk.

Diego saw movement inside the fort. Seconds later, Sienna's head poked out. She looked right at him. Her forehead and nose were all scrunched up as she crawled out completely and made her way over to him. As she stood in front of him, her inquisitive eyes watched him like a hawk.

"Uncle Diego, what are you doing?" She asked him.

He raised his eyebrows then glanced down at the babies. Their little grunts and snorts as they suckled their bottles clearly told anyone what they were doing.

"Feeding Kelsey and Kensi."

Her eyes widened.

"You're doing it wrong," she told him.

"I am?" He asked as he wrinkled his forehead then looked down. From their half-empty bottles, it appeared to him that he was doing it correctly.

She walked closer and ran her hand gently over Kelsey's dark hair. It was amazing how gentle and compassionate all the kids were with the babies. She met his eyes.

"You need to take your shirt off."

It was Diego's turn to look at her wide-eyed. "I do?"

Sienna's little head nodded. "The babies can't suck your boobies if they can't find them. What are you feeding them? They can only eat what comes out of Aunt Tenley's boobies." Her eyes got even bigger, and Diego braced himself because he knew the curious six-year-old wasn't finished, and quite frankly, he was a little frightened of what may come out of that little mouth of hers next.

"Did you use that machine that Aunt Tenley uses?" She wrinkled her nose again as if she was thinking. "You know the one that sucks the milk from her boobies."

Diego felt mortified. He didn't want to think or hear any more about Aunt Tenley's boobies. Then he smiled to himself. He could really fuck with Potter.

He honestly didn't know how to respond. He was just going to tell her that Tenley provided the milk to him, which she did, but then a snort of laughter came from the kitchen. When he glanced over, he found Campbell leaning against the counter that separated the two rooms. She had her hand over her mouth, and he knew she was hiding the big smile on her face. In return, he squinted his eyes playfully at her.

Campbell put the last plate away in the cabinet then took one last look around the kitchen to make sure everything was wiped down and back in its place.

She was sure going to miss this kitchen when it was time for her to leave. Who was she kidding? She was going to miss everything about this place, including her number one. She was falling hard for Diego and seeing him interact with the kids made her grow fonder of him. He was everything she'd imagine a man should be. He was sweet, compassionate, protective; what wasn't there to not like.

But just like her life so far, all good things must come to an end. The thought of walking away from him and the friendships she'd established caused a pang to hit her belly. The sound of the kids laughing at something in the movie caused her to push the negative thoughts aside for now. She'd worry about it when the time came. For now, she'd continue doing what she had been doing—enjoying the present.

She walked into the living room and was stopped in her tracks, seeing the two babies snuggled against Diego's ample chest. That sight alone sent her ovaries into overdrive. She was glad to see that Sienna and her curious mind had gone back inside the fort to finish watching the movie. That little girl was a firecracker, but a cute one. Poor Irish was going to have his hands full with that one.

She picked up Kelsey first since she was starting to squirm. Her little eyelids kept closing, and she was fighting the sleep. She burped her then changed her diaper before putting her into her pajamas. She had already set up their pack n plays before dinner so that it would be an easy transition when bedtime came.

After getting Kelsey settled, she turned to get Kensi and found Diego watching her.

"I didn't mean to disturb you. I wanted to get the babies settled in for the night."

Without a word, he stood up.

"What do you need me to do?" He asked.

"You don't have to do anything; just relax."

"I want to. I missed out on this with my nieces and nephews."

"Okay. Bring her over to the pack n play and lay her on the little changing pad. We'll change her diaper first."

Campbell went through the steps of diaper changing with Diego. She wanted to laugh at how serious he was about it. She swore if he had a pen and paper, he would've taken notes.

Once he mastered Kensi's diaper, she gave him the little one-piece to put on her. Kensi fell back asleep as they were changing her. Diego set her inside the pack n play and made sure the light above them wasn't too bright.

Once the babies were settled and fast asleep, they walked back to the couch and sat down.

"Was your head bothering you earlier?" She asked him.

He looked away, and for a moment, she thought she had overstepped again, but he looked back at her.

"It did, but I think it was just a tension headache. I took some Tylenol, and that seemed to do the trick."

She nodded her head but knew he disliked talking about his injury, so she changed the subject.

"The kids seemed to have a good time. Did they tell you about the letters they wrote to their parents?"

"No. What type of letters?"

"Each of them was telling me in their words how they ended up in Virginia Beach. That conversation then led to what they were thankful for. If you think about it, where would Cody be without Frost? I mean, he has Autumn, but I can see a lot of Frost in Cody even though they aren't blood-related. Then you have Sienna. Irish deserves major kudos for the responsibility he took on. Not many people in his position would even consider taking in a child, even if they were family. Then factor in Bailey, who loves that little girl like her own. And last but not least, Alejandra. Her story is truly touching. You had a little girl who had her life and family ripped from her. If it weren't for Tenley and Potter, who knows where she would've ended up. Anyway, afterward, I asked them if they wanted to write a note to their parents telling them what they had just told me, and they all said yes."

Diego smiled. "That's awesome, Campbell. I can already tell you that Potter and Tenley, Frost and Autumn, and Irish and Bailey will all appreciate it."

Campbell didn't tell Diego, but she joined the kids and wrote a letter to her parents even though neither one was around to read it. It was something maybe someday she'd get the chance to visit their graves and read it to them.

"I wanted to run something by you," Diego said.

"What's that?"

"How do you feel about taking a trip this weekend?"

She looked at him. "Where would we go?"

"My mom's throwing a big party for my dad for his birthday. I haven't been home in a while, and since I have the time, I thought I'd go. I told my mom about you, and she's dying to meet you."

Campbell wondered precisely what he had told his mom. "You told your mom about me?"

Diego's eyes widened, and he quickly followed up his statement. "I didn't tell her about your situation if that's what you were wondering."

She nibbled her lip. It was becoming a bad habit that she needed to break, before she chewed a hole in her lip. Of course, her first instinct was to say yes, but being around his family and knowing the feelings she had for him, she'd feel awkward. Maybe it wasn't such a great idea.

"I don't know. I mean, that's your time to spend with your family, and even you said it yourself that it's been a while since you were home."

"I want you to come. Believe me, having you around will be a blessing. Plus, I'd love to show you around."

She grinned. "You make it hard to say no."

He smiled. "Good."

"Where are we heading then?"

"Texas."

Yee-haw, she thought to herself.

CHAPTER SEVENTEEN

Diego and Campbell boarded the Boeing 737 bound for Brownsville South Padre Island International Airport late Friday evening. As they took their seats in the last row in the back of the plane, Diego noticed that Campbell had been extremely quiet since they arrived at the airport. She had been fine the night before and seemed excited about the trip when they talked about it. But now, she appeared timid, and he was unsure as to what brought that on.

He watched her as she seemed fascinated looking out the window at the ground workers loading and unloading bags from the nearby planes.

He touched her shoulder, and she tilted her head back to look at him. In doing so, her strawberry waves fell over her arm.

"Are you okay?" He asked.

She nodded her head, gave him a faint smile then turned back to the window.

From experience with his sisters and the other women from the team, he knew that something was bothering her. Women always said they were fine, when they really weren't. He never understood that.

As the plane taxied out to the runway, the captain came over the speakers, introduced himself, and informed the passengers that they were second in line for takeoff.

After a minute or two of sitting idle, the plane started to move again, making its way onto the runway. In the distance, he could hear the roar of the prior plane's engines as it took off.

Taking another look at Campbell, she was still quiet and still looking out the window, so he leaned his head back. Just as he closed his eyes, he felt a small delicate hand cover his. His eyes popped open, and he became concerned when Campbell was looking at him with tears in her eyes.

He squeezed her hand and leaned over.

"Campbell, what's wrong?"

She gave him that soft, gentle smile of hers. "I'm fine—just a little sad. I'm sorry I wasn't honest with you earlier. I probably should've told you before we boarded that I've never flown before."

Oh shit!

"Campbell—"

She pressed her finger to his lips and smiled. "Let me finish." As she started to talk, the roar of the plane's engines began to grow louder, signaling they were getting ready to take off. "I'm not afraid of flying if that's what you're worried about."

He squeezed her hand. "As soon as we get into the air, you're going to explain what has you feeling sad."

She nodded her head and gripped his hand tighter as the plane began to race down the runway.

As the plane lifted off the ground, he heard the faint gasp that left her lips, and he grinned. She had her forehead pressed against the window as she watched the plane climb higher and higher.

When the plane finally started to level off, Diego thought she'd let go of his hand, but she didn't. And he was okay with that. He loved holding her hand.

"It's beautiful up here," she said as she looked out the window at the white fluffy looking clouds and blue sky, with the sun setting in an aesthetic performance. He leaned over to look, and she was right; it was a beautiful sight, but with her in it.

She looked over her shoulder and gave him a cheeky grin that just about melted his heart. Before realizing what he was doing, he moved a stray piece of her hair behind her ear.

"Your smile is even more beautiful," he told her. He must have shocked her because she lowered her eyes, and her cheeks turned a little pink. But then she turned the tables on him when she leaned over and pressed her warm wet lips gently against his cheek.

"Thank you, Diego." She whispered, and her breath hit the shell of his ear, and fuck if those warm puffs of air didn't send a lightning bolt zipping through his body. This woman had a significant effect on his libido.

Further surprising him, she laid her head against his shoulder. She stayed that way for a few minutes before looking up at him.

"My dad didn't take many vacations because he was always working—even before my mom died. We never really took trips unless they were for my dance recitals, but even then, we drove. After mom died, he always promised me that he and I would take a trip somewhere and that we'd fly. But we never got that opportunity." A tear slipped out of her eye and rolled halfway down her cheek before Diego wiped it away with his thumb.

"You've come to mean so much to me. More than you'll ever know," she admitted to him. She wanted him to know. He needed to know.

He wiped another tear from her face, and he felt himself become emotional.

"You deserve all the happiness you can find in this world," he told her, looking deep into her eyes.

"I am happy. Thanks to you and your generosity."

He grinned and ran his knuckles down her cheek. Things were definitely changing between them, and Diego was thrilled.

"I'm happy that you accepted and trusted me."

"I'll always trust you."

CHAPTER EIGHTEEN

The following morning, Diego walked into the kitchen and found his mom doing what she loved—cooking. She was an amazing woman and mother. She had risked everything, including alienating her family when she moved to the United States at just nineteen years old, seeking shelter with the man she fell in love with.

He walked over and kissed her cheek before grabbing a cup of coffee.

"Morning, momma."

She smiled. "Good morning, Mateo."

He shook his head and chuckled. She never called him by his nickname. In fact, she had been pissed at first when she found out the reasoning behind the name. She had thought that his drill instructor at the time had meant it as a racist term, but then when he explained that it was his instructor's kid who called him that she then understood and thought it was cute he was nicknamed after Diego from *Go, Diego, Go.*

He noticed it was unusually quiet in the house. He looked at the clock and was surprised. Normally by now, no matter what day it was, his mom's house and farm were awake. But since his momma was throwing a big party today, he was shocked and a little concerned about where everyone was. Any other time his sisters would be in the kitchen helping their mom with the food preparations.

"Is everyone still asleep?" He asked before taking a sip of the strong java.

He and Campbell had arrived late last night, so they had missed everyone except for his mom and dad. That was the hard part of getting a chance to travel home—the visit was never long enough. Today would be the only full day he'd get with his family. But at least with the party being held at his parents' house, he'd get to see everyone, and everyone would also get the opportunity to meet Campbell, who he hoped would play a massive role in his future. He cared deeply for the shy, strawberry blonde pixie. To him she was a breath of fresh air.

His mom grinned. "It seems your guest has made quite the impression on your sisters. They're all out with the animals."

Diego walked over to the French doors that led out onto the wraparound porch. He watched as Campbell laughed and spoke with his four sisters and their kids. He couldn't hide his smile when she bent down and picked up the miniature black and white goat and held it against her chest.

His mom walked over and stood next to him, watching the girls.

"She's a beautiful woman. I can tell she has a big heart. I'll admit, I like her a lot." She raised her eyebrows, and Diego looked down at her. He ran his hand over his head and groaned.

"Mom…"

She held her hands up. "Hey, I'm just saying that I would approve. How you feel about her is your thing. But, from someone sitting on the sideline watching, that lovely woman only has eyes for you, and if I'm not mistaken, you only have eyes for her."

Diego looked back outside, focusing on Campbell. Could she truly be the one for him? He wanted what his mom and dad had—love, loyalty, trust, and respect.

"You've never approved of anyone that I brought home to meet you. But what's not to like about her?"

When his mom's eyes lit up, and a slow smile spread across her face, he realized that he had walked right into her trap. He just admitted he had feelings for her. *Son of a bitch!*

He took a sip of his coffee, and his mom laughed.

"How did you two meet?" She asked, and he walked over to the large island where she went back to making tamales. He pulled a stool out and sat down, then explained how he met Campbell Rogers.

"Do you think this guy is still looking for her?" She asked, appearing very concerned.

"I honestly don't know. So far, it's been quiet. As I said, my commander is friends with Campbell's former employer. He's been somewhat keeping us informed if he hears anything. But it's been radio silent, and I'm not sure if that's a good thing or a bad thing."

"He sounds like he is obsessed with her. Men like that don't give up too easily. Promise me you'll keep her safe, Mateo."

Diego smiled. "That is my intention. I just need to make some adjustments if I get cleared."

"If?" She asked with a raised eyebrow.

"My return isn't guaranteed, Mom."

"When do you find out?"

"Monday morning."

"What do you think the final verdict will be? You, of all people, know your body better than anyone."

He blew out a breath. "My appointment with the physician went well. According to him, I'm ready. But it's up to the board to put me back in."

Diego heard the horses in the distance, and he got an idea. He'd rather be involved in something fun than sitting around drowning in his sorrows.

"You don't need any help, do you?"

She raised an eyebrow at him. "Why do you ask?"

"Campbell has never been horseback riding. I was thinking about taking her up the trails and then stopping at the lake."

She smiled wide. "Go have fun. I have your sisters here to help get things ready. Plus, your dad will be home shortly from the store, and he can get the grill ready. The lake this time of the year is gorgeous."

Remembering the conversation he and Campbell had the other night about being thankful for their parents, Diego walked around the island and pulled his mom into a big hug.

"Thank you, Mom. For everything."

She looked up at him. "I'm so proud of you and what you've become. Even though it frightens me what you and your teammates get into."

He smiled. "We look after each other."

She patted his chest. "Go on, go have some fun with my future daughter-in-law," she teased, and Diego rolled his eyes.

He was about to walk away when his mom called his name.

"Mateo?"

"Yeah?"

"All joking aside, I meant what I said—she's a keeper."

He grinned. "I know, Mom."

Before he turned back around, he swore he saw her do a fist pump in the air. He shook his head and smiled.

Campbell couldn't believe how much she enjoyed farm life. At least at Diego's parents' farm. The farms she grew up around were commercial farms. Diego's parents' farm reminded her more of a family farm with various animals that weren't raised and sold for commercial purposes. All the animals were part of the family.

She was glad she had woken up early and had the opportunity to sit and talk with Diego's mom, Emilia, before the house started to fill with Diego's family. The way that Emilia spoke about her only son told Campbell how much Emilia loved Diego. She was a woman who cared deeply about family values. She was full of love and had a huge heart, just as a mother should have. She wanted to melt in Emilia's arms when Emilia hugged her upon hearing about the passing of her parents.

On the other hand, Diego's sisters, Mirabella, Isla, Maya, and Amada, were a force to be reckoned with, but in a good way. They were all friendly and loved to hug, making Campbell feel as if she was a part of their family. At one point, she felt her heart sink a little. Watching Diego's sisters interact with each other made her wonder if that could've been her and Lizzy at one time. As angry as she was at Lizzy for her actions, Campbell still loved her sister.

She bent down to pet her new friend, Oreo, the most adorable black and white miniature goat. If she could, she'd smuggle it back to Virginia.

"You are just the cutest little thing." She told the goat as he bleated, bringing a smile to her face.

"I don't know. I think Oreo has some competition." The deep, male voice behind her said.

She stood and spun around, shocked that she hadn't heard Diego sneak up behind her.

"What?" She asked.

Diego took a few steps and closed the distance between them. She looked up at him. God, he was good-looking, and so sweet.

He reached down and tucked a strand of hair behind her ear. It was a thing he liked to do.

"I said that Oreo has competition on being the cutest."

She wrinkled her nose and looked around. "Who's the competition?"

He stared deep into her eyes. "You."

Campbell was stunned, speechless. She wasn't sure how to reply. She opened her mouth to say something, anything, but nothing came out. It was like her voice had been stolen. Holy crap. Had he just made the first move?

As if sensing her shock, Diego smiled. "I was thinking about taking a ride before everyone gets here. Would you like to join me?"

She was still staring at him, and she only caught a little of what he asked her. Something about a ride? She shook her head.

"I'm sorry. What did you just ask me?"

He snickered. "I asked if you wanted to go for a ride with me?"

"Where to?"

"Up to the lake."

"Sure. How are we getting there?"

Diego pointed at something behind her. When she turned around, she saw another beautiful creature walking towards the fence. The dark brown horse seemed to perk up at the sight of Diego.

She turned back toward Diego. "I've never ridden a horse before."

He grinned. "I know. But you'll be fine."

He went to walk toward the horse when she grabbed his arm. "Diego, seriously. I don't know if I can ride a horse."

He cupped her cheeks. "Campbell, you'll be fine. You'll be riding with me." He kissed her forehead, and she thought her knees would buckle from under her. "Come on. I'll introduce you to Hurricane."

Hurricane? Oh, God. The name alone didn't give her a warm or fuzzy feeling.

༄

Once he got Hurricane saddled up, and Campbell mounted the horse, they rode through the trails as he pointed out different scenery. He closed his eyes and took a deep breath. He missed this. But he was also glad he was able to share it with Campbell.

He pressed his chest against her back as he held her around the waist with one arm. As they entered a large clearing and the lake came into view, he heard her gasp, and she looked up over her shoulder at him.

"Diego, this is gorgeous."

He followed her sight. She wasn't lying; it was a sight. The lake was smooth as glass—not a ripple in sight. The reflection of the sky and surrounding foliage on the water made it look like a painting.

He dismounted then helped Campbell down.

"Gosh. How do you manage to leave this place?" She asked him as she continued to look all around her.

"It's hard. I come up here every time I'm home. It's a great place to just come to and think." He admitted.

"How often do you get to come home?"

"Not as much as I'd like to. But it's the career I chose."

"You like it? Your career?"

"I love it."

"It's dangerous, though."

He grinned. "Any career could be dangerous."

She nudged his arm playfully. "You know what I meant." Then she got serious.

"Are you scared?"

"Of what?"

"Of the decision you'll get on Monday."

"Yeah. I am. The SEALs are my life. Those guys are my family. I don't know what I'd do without them."

She reached out and placed her hand on his arm. "Those men love you too, and they'll always be your family no matter the outcome."

"What happens if they don't clear you? I mean, what will you do?"

He took a deep breath and looked out at the water. That was something he didn't like to think about because he was trying to stay positive.

"They would most likely offer me a desk job. But I could never accept that."

"Why not?"

"From being out in the field, I know what I'd be missing out on, and it would drive me crazy to have to stay back and be a desk clerk. Not that there's anything wrong with it. But that just isn't me. Most likely, I'd seek an honorable discharge and go work for Tink's security company."

She caught him off guard when she took his hand and moved, so she was standing in front of him as she looked up at him. "I'm feeling some pretty positive vibes."

"Are you?" He said with a sly grin and tugged on her hand, pulling her closer until they were almost touching. The atmosphere in the air crackled between them. He watched her chest rise and fall with each breath she took.

Using his knuckles, he gently caressed her cheek as he stared deep into her hazel eyes. She was beautiful, she was full of life, and she was going to be his.

She licked her lips as they held each other's gaze. Slowly Diego bent his head. And right on cue, as if she knew what he was seeking, she closed her eyes. He felt the anticipation of their kiss grow. Just when he was a hair's breadth away from her lips, he heard his sister's voice echo from across the lake.

"There you two are!"

Campbell's eyes popped open, and immediately she took a step back. And just like that, the moment was gone, and he swore to himself.

Mirabella always had the worst fucking timing. He waved as she drove the ATV closer.

He looked at Campbell, who again was biting on her lip. He couldn't get a read on her, but he wondered what she was thinking.

Mirabella pulled up next to them and cut the engine.

"What's up?" He asked her as he gave her the stink eye.

"Mom said you were bringing Campbell up here." She turned toward Campbell and smiled. "My mom is completely freaking out right now because she forgot to ask you if you like Mexican food. She realized that after she prepared a Mexican feast. She said she can whip up something if you don't."

Campbell smiled. "Mexican is fine. In fact, I'm looking forward to having authentic Mexican food. I've had it at restaurants but never homecooked."

"Oh, you're going to love our mom's food. And make sure you save room for dessert. She made Pineapple Empanadas and Tres leches cake."

"Tres leches cake?" Campbell questioned, and Diego answered.

"It's a very moist cake. It's a cake drizzled with three different kinds of milk—evaporated milk, sweetened condensed milk, and heavy cream. That's what makes it so sweet and decadent. It's the bomb. Mom tops hers with a dollop of whipped cream and fresh strawberries."

Campbell grinned. "That sounds delicious."

"Because it is," Mirabella said. "When are you guys heading back? Uncle Ramos and Aunt Juanita, along with the rest of the family, should be arriving soon. Dad has the grill fired up and the music playing."

Diego glanced at Campbell, and he could tell she was a little uncomfortable. The culprit being they had almost gotten caught kissing by his sister.

"We're getting ready to head back now."

"Oh." Mirabella looked at Campbell. "Would you like to ride with me?"

Campbell looked at Diego, and he could tell she was torn between going with him and wanting to please his sister, so he helped her out. He smiled. "Go ahead. I'll be along shortly."

"Are you sure you don't mind?"

"No. It's fine." And it was, because it would give him a little bit of time to contemplate his life and future.

He watched Campbell slide into the empty seat next to Mirabella. As Mirabella stepped on the gas and started to drive away, Campbell turned back to look at him. The sincere look in her eyes was what he was looking for, and when she offered a small smile, he knew it was all going to be okay.

Diego couldn't remember when last he'd had this much fun at a family get-together. During the day, he didn't think that one more person could fit on the deck. And the backyard was lined with tables full of family and friends. There were even some friends who stopped by to say hi when they heard he was home. It was definitely a memorable day.

He was sitting on the porch swing with his dad as they watched the girls dancing. Diego felt terrible for throwing Campbell to the wolves. He had accidentally mentioned to his sister, Isla, about Campbell being a dancer—well, used to be, though he was still curious about her ability to dance. She and Fred had both commented that her broken leg had ruined her career, but from what he witnessed in his kitchen last week, she was far from a ruined dancer.

They were dancing to some country song that Diego had heard of, but the girls knew it. It was a line dance. They definitely had acquired a large audience, especially Campbell. He noticed his male cousins watching her earlier, and he made it a point to let them know that she was off-limits.

As soon as the song ended, everyone started cheering and clapping. Campbell was grinning from ear to ear, and the sight warmed Diego's heart. Here was a woman who, when they first met, was closed off and timid. And now, to see her smiling and interacting with his family and complete strangers showed just how far along she'd come in such a short time.

He smiled as she walked toward him and his dad. Diego could see she was sweating, so he reached over the back of the swing to grab a bottle of water, and he handed it to her.

"Thank you," she said before twisting the cap off and guzzling about half the bottle.

"Dang, girl, can you dance to any type of music?" Diego's dad asked her.

She lifted one of her shoulders. "Most of the time. As long as you have some rhythm, you can dance to any beat."

Once his dad got up to talk to some friends, Diego patted the empty seat next to him. "Have a seat and take a load off," he told her.

She didn't hesitate. She took another sip of water before she set it down on the table next to the swing. She closed her eyes.

"I could sit out here all day," she said, and he grinned.

"Are you having fun?" He asked.

"I am. Thank you for inviting me. Your family is wonderful."

"My mom always used to say that being a family meant that you're part of something truly wonderful. It means that you'll love and be loved for the rest of your life."

Her lips lifted in a smile. "That sounds beautiful."

As they sat there talking to one another, other people joined them. Then before long, it started to get late, and most of the guests had left. Night had fallen, and the two of them were still sitting on the swing. It had been a long day. But Campbell wouldn't have traded it for the world. Getting to spend the day like this was amazing.

Diego turned sideways in the swing so that he faced her. "You dance beautifully."

"Thank you."

"Both you and Fred said that when you broke your leg it ruined your dancing career, but you seemed fine when you were dancing with my sisters earlier. I also watched you dance in our kitchen the night I scared you into breaking the glass."

She dropped her gaze and stared at her hands that were in her lap. How could she explain it—that getting injured made her realize that dancing wasn't who she was.

"My mom was a dancer, and so was Lizzy. Like most little girls, I wanted to follow in my mom's footsteps and be a ballerina like her. After Mom died, a part of my dancing died. I no longer had that drive, but I did it because of my dad. I think him watching me dance gave him back a part of my mom. I only continued because I saw how happy he was at my recitals, and I know it was because it reminded him of mom. After dad died, I don't know why I kept dancing, maybe because it got me out of the house and away from Mitchell. I don't really know. All I know is that after Mitchell broke my leg, even if I wanted to continue dancing, I couldn't. You're right, I danced with your sisters, and I danced to a few songs in your kitchen, but my leg can't hold up dancing for many hours during a show. And honestly, I don't want to. If I dance, I want to dance for me, not anybody else. Tonight was magical, and it felt wonderful being me and dancing on my terms."

She took a big breath and exhaled. *Damn, that had felt good to get out*, she thought to herself. She looked up at Diego and absorbed his dark brown eyes.

"Does that make sense?" She asked him.

He cupped her cheek and smiled. "It makes perfect sense."

Campbell felt herself leaning into his touch, and before she knew it, Diego had her wrapped up in his muscular arms with her head resting against his chest. Listening and feeling his heartbeat beneath her cheek, she felt happy, protected, and content.

Diego couldn't get enough of Campbell, and apparently, neither could his family. He received a thumbs up from everyone that mattered.

Holding her in his arms sent a sensation through his body that he'd never felt. Campbell was special.

He felt her stir, and he released her for her to stand up, and he followed.

"I guess I'll see you in the morning," she told him.

"We'll head out around oh eight hundred."

She furrowed her eyebrows. "Huh?"

He chuckled, remembering that not everyone was up to speed with military time. "Eight o'clock."

"Oh. Gotcha." She said with a grin. "Maybe one day you can give me a crash course on military time."

He laughed. "That I can do."

"Good night," she said before turning to go into the house.

He watched her, not wanting her to go. Suddenly she turned back around, and before he knew it, she flung her arms around his neck and hugged him.

Surprised by her move, but not one to miss an opportunity, he hugged her back.

"What's this for?" He asked even though he didn't care. He was just happy to feel her in his arms. It was where she belonged.

She let go, took a step backward, and slid her hands in the back pocket of her jeans. When she looked up at him, he didn't miss the redness along her cheeks. Her eyes were a bit glassy, and he wondered if something was wrong. But she seemed happy.

"I know I've said this many times already, but thank you. This trip means more to me than you'll ever know. Getting to know your family has been wonderful. You should be very grateful for what you have. Don't ever let it go."

"Family is one thing I don't take for granted. They're my life. That includes my family back home as well."

There was a commotion inside, and when Diego glanced through the kitchen window, he saw his mom putting things away. He shook his head in amazement. He'd been cock-blocked twice in one day by his own family.

"I guess we should turn in," he told her.

"Guess so. Goodnight, Diego."
"Night, Campbell."

CHAPTER NINETEEN

Monday morning Campbell stood next to Diego's truck. After about an hour of begging him to let her come with him to his meeting, he finally relented and agreed, but told her she would not be allowed past a certain point. She didn't care, just as long as she was the first to know the outcome. She agreed she would stay in the truck, and she brought along the tablet Diego had gotten her to pass the time. But she was too nervous and couldn't concentrate. It was just about to hit the ninetieth minute when a black truck and a green jeep pulled into the parking spots next to hers. She recognized them immediately. It was Ace and Stitch. She wondered what they were doing here since Diego had made it clear he didn't want any of the team here. She was even more shocked when the doors opened to both vehicles and saw it wasn't just Ace and Stitch but the entire team.

Ace walked over to her. "Hey, Campbell."

She smiled. Ace was a large man. Well, they all were, but he carried himself with confidence that showed leadership and authority.

"Hi. What are you all doing here?"

"Why wouldn't we be here? Diego's part of the team, and we stick by our brothers."

"How are you doing?" He asked her.

"Okay, I guess." She ran her palms along her jeans.

He lifted one of his eyebrows. "Just, okay?"

"Okay, nervous," she admitted.

Ace grinned. "That's understandable. But I'm sure Diego appreciates your support."

"It's the least I can do for him after everything he has done for me."

She looked at her watch again and wondered how much longer it was going to be. Ace and the guys told her they would talk to her later before heading inside the same building she saw Diego disappear into.

She climbed back inside the truck. She leaned her head back and closed her eyes. It was a beautiful spring day, and she smiled as a light breeze blew in from the open window.

Ever since her mom passed away, anytime a light breeze would blow in, she always believed it was her mom saying hello and letting her know that she was still there watching over her.

She wondered if that were the case right now. It was strange, but she felt at peace and felt she was where she needed to be.

The breeze moved on, and she heard the sound of gravel crunching. When she opened her eyes and saw Diego walking toward her with a huge smile on his face, she knew he was coming with good news.

She hopped out of the truck and met him in front of it.

"Judging from that smile on your face, I'm guessing you got the news you wanted."

"I'm back in business!"

He surprised her when he lifted her into the air and twirled her around as she clung to his shoulders and laughed.

The others came out of the building and joined them as he set her down. She didn't miss the smiles and winks some of the guys gave her as if knowing she liked Diego.

"Welcome back officially!" Ace told him and slapped him on the back. The others congratulated him as well.

Campbell watched in awe as they all interacted. Seeing how they supported one another made her realize how unique their little family really was. It was just as Alex explained. They were brothers in arms.

"The commander wants a word with us, then Alex planned a little celebration at Bayside." Ace announced.

"Little?" Stitch asked.

Ace held his hands up. "Those were her words, not mine." They all laughed, knowing Alex never did anything small.

Diego looked at Campbell. "I don't know how long we'll be. Sometimes these chats can take a while." He reached into his pocket and pulled out his keys. "Take the truck to Bayside, and I'll grab a ride with one of the guys."

At first, she felt a little jilted, but she pushed it aside, knowing he had a lot on his mind and much to celebrate.

As she climbed into the driver's seat and started the engine, she realized that she had more important things to think about—starting with where she was going to live. She was also going to need a job. The worst part was going to be saying goodbye to Diego.

With a heavy heart, she drove the short distance and pulled into the parking lot of Bayside. Before she got out, she tried to give herself a pep talk saying everything happens for a reason and that she'd be okay, no matter what happened. But deep down, she wasn't sure she believed it.

Diego sat in Derek's office with the rest of the team. The Intel community had been monitoring some chatter coming out of Sweden. It wasn't a surprise as they had all been anticipating they were going to get the call to head out.

In partnership with the U.S., Sweden's Intelligence Agency uncovered a small terrorist cell in the heart of Stockholm—Sweden's capital.

Initial intel suggested that the cell was targeting the two locations, the Parliament House and U.S. Embassy. Sources on the ground and close to the situation asked the Defense Intelligence Agency to raise the threat warning to high. Inside the military, the DOD Force Protection Level was raised to Delta status, meaning that terrorist action against a specific location was imminent.

Derek explained they were waiting to hear from Sweden's Military Command but told them to be ready to head out at a moment's notice.

Once Derek dismissed the team, Diego was stopped in the hall by Bear and his team. They were all congratulating him when Derek approached.

"Diego…I need to talk to you. Got a minute?"

"Sure."

Diego looked at the guys and told them he'd meet them at Bayside, but Ace reminded him that he gave his truck to Campbell. They told Diego that they'd wait for him outside.

He followed Derek back to his office. When they entered, Derek shut the door behind them.

"Go ahead and have a seat."

"What's going on?"

"I got a call last night from Fred. He said that Mitchell sold the mine."

"What?"

"I know, strange, and not something we expected."

"Why?"

"The only thing we can find is that he was coming under some heavy criticism from the federal regulators on how he operated the business. He had to pay a seven hundred thousand dollar fine for code violations stemming from the accident that killed Campbell's dad."

"Damn."

"That's not all. It seems he also left town."

Diego raised his eyebrows. "Like for good?"

Derek shrugged his shoulders. "We aren't certain, but he did put his house up for sale, and nobody has seen him around."

"I know that look. There's something else."

"After I got off the phone with Fred, I called Tink. He did a little investigating, and it appears that Mitchell invested a large sum of money into a mining company in Russia."

"Russia? What in the hell do they mine? Why there?"

"Tink believes diamonds. But we don't know for sure."

"Does Tink think Mitchell moved out of the country, specifically to Russia?"

"Again, we can't confirm it. He has some of his people still digging for information. I just wanted you to know. You can let Campbell know.

"I will. Thank you for the update."

Derek smirked, "Go on and get outta here. I know Alex planned a celebration for you."

"Are you coming?"

"Yeah. I just need to finish up a few tasks first."

As soon as Diego stepped foot inside Bayside, he scanned the room. He found Alex fiddling with balloons and walked over. When she turned around, she smiled and hugged him.

"Congratulations."

"Thanks." He looked around again, hoping to find Campbell. Where the hell was she?

"If you're looking for your other half, she's out on the beach."

Diego snorted a laugh. "Did she say anything when she got here?" He asked Alex, and she shook her head.

"Nothing that stood out. She told us you guys got called into Derek's office and that you'd be here when you all got here. But that was it. Is everything okay?"

He shook his head. "I honestly don't know." He looked at Alex. "I'll be right back."

Before he could take a step, Alex grabbed his arm, stopping him. "I like her, Diego."

He grinned, knowing all the ladies had taken an instant liking to Campbell. That even went for all the guys as well.

"I do too, Alex."

She smiled. "Then go get her. She's the missing piece to our team here at home."

He never thought about it that way. He was the only single one left. Alex was right. Campbell would complete their family.

Campbell dug her toes into the sand. She was going to miss this. After never having been to the beach, she had fallen in love with it.

But she knew her time was limited and that she would need to start looking at other avenues. Especially now that Diego would be returning to his team. She was thrilled for him. She knew how much being on the team meant to him. She could hear the pride and love for the SEALs every time he spoke about it.

It saddened her because she felt that she had found herself for the first time in her life. She knew that she would be okay with time no matter where she ended up, because she wasn't the same person she was when she first arrived just over a month ago. Gone was the timid naïve girl, and in her place was a more confident and assertive woman.

The hardest part she was going to endure was leaving Diego. She wasn't sure if he realized it, but she had given her heart to him, and she didn't know if she would ever be able to get it back.

"It's beautiful out here."

Campbell twisted her head around when she heard Diego's deep voice from behind her.

He stepped closer, and she shielded her eyes from the sun when she looked up at him. He looked sharp and happy.

"Hey." She greeted him and tried to put a smile on her face. He didn't say anything at first and continued to stare at her.

"What are you doing out here by yourself?"

She shrugged her shoulders. "Thinking."

"Thinking about what?"

"What's next for me."

"And what's next for you?"

"I don't know yet. I'm considering my options on where I'll end up when I leave here."

He squeezed her shoulders. "Wait, you're thinking about leaving?"

"Well, since you're back on active duty, it only makes sense for me to move on."

He cocked his head to one side. "What does that have to do with you staying or leaving?"

"I just figured. I was a job for you, Diego."

"Were you? Because I never once thought of you as a job." He glanced back out at the ocean before turning his brown eyes to her. "I don't want you to leave."

"You don't?"

"Hell no, woman. Unless you tell me right now that you want to leave, I'm not letting you go."

Her heart started to race, and she shook her head. Her emotions were beginning to grab hold of her. "I don't want to leave. I feel like I finally found my home here. But…"

She stared up into his eyes. They were full of fire. He tugged her closer and cupped her cheek with his large palm.

"But what, Campbell?"

"I've experienced so many firsts with you—the beach, flying in a plane, horseback riding."

"Is that all?" He asked, and she shook her head.

"Love. I experienced what it's like to love someone."

"What are you saying, Campbell?"

Right at that moment, a gust of wind blew in off the ocean, catching her hair and sending it all over the place, and she couldn't help but smile, and she thought of it as a sign from her mom telling her to go for it.

"I love you, Diego. Somehow, someway, I fell in love with you."

He stared at her for a moment. His silence made her feel like a fool for blurting that out. What if he didn't feel the same for her?

"Diego—"

He silenced her with his finger pressed against her lips. He broke eye contact with her and stared out at the water.

"Today is one of the happiest days of my life, but I'm not satisfied."

She looked back up at him, confused by his statement. "Why? This is what you wanted. You're back on the team."

He shook his head. "Life isn't just about me." He turned to face her; his dark brown eyes held her gaze. He reached for her hand and lifted it against his chest. She could feel his strong heartbeat.

"I don't want to tell you. Let me show you."

He slid one of his hands under her silky hair and gripped the back of her neck, tugging her towards him before lowering his mouth to hers. Before he kissed her, he smiled against her lips. "For the record, I love you too." She heard her own intake of breath before he crashed his lips onto hers and kissed her with passion and so much heat that she felt her toes curl into the sand. He delved his tongue in her mouth and licked every inch of it he could. He picked her up, and she straddled his waist as she wrapped her arms around his neck and hugged him.

In the distance, she could hear people hooting and hollering, and when Diego turned them around, there stood the entire team and their families on the deck cheering for them. It was a moment she'd never forget and one she would treasure forever.

Diego started walking them back up to the restaurant.

"What are you doing?" She asked, trying to get down, but he kept a firm grip around her.

"Taking you back to our house and our bed where you belong and where I can lay you out and love your body as it should be."

"What? What about your party?"

"Oh, believe me, they won't miss us—too much."

As he climbed the steps with her in his arms, he said, "I hope you had a nutritious lunch because I don't plan to break for dinner for a couple of hours. At least, not until I get my fill of you."

"Oh my God. You are crazy!" she told him as they walked past their friends.

"Crazy for you, sweetheart." And he smacked her ass as he carried her from the bar, with his teammates and their women cheering them on. She swore she heard one of the guys say, "I guess it's a party for two back at Diego's."

Diego glanced over at Campbell in the passenger seat as they drove to the house. She was sitting quietly with her hands clasped on her lap, looking straight ahead. He reached over and took her hand and brought it up to his lips. She turned and smiled at him. It was hard to keep his eyes on the road because she was that beautiful to look at.

"You okay? You seem a little quiet."

She nodded her head then looked back to staring out the windshield. At first, he was concerned she was having second thoughts, but he immediately realized the issue when he saw her squirm in the seat. She was sexually aroused, and he felt his cock grow.

Back at the house, neither said a word as they got out of the truck. Diego met her at the front, placed his hand on her lower back, and guided her to the front door. As soon as they both made it through the door and secured all the locks, he couldn't take it anymore. Watching her squirm and hearing her sigh all the way home had him so fired up, he was on the verge of exploding.

She went to walk past him, but he gripped her waist, turned her around, and lifted her, pressing her back up against the door. He could feel the heat from her pussy through his jeans. He took her mouth hard in a deep kiss. She gripped the hem of his shirt and lifted it over his head. It was wild and intense. She quickly moved to his jeans, undoing the button and sliding down the zipper, all while Diego continued the assault to her mouth. He stopped her just as she was about to push his jeans down.

He set her back on her feet. Slowly he popped the button to her jeans and slid them down her legs, helping her out of them. He went to his knees, pausing briefly before running his hands up her thighs, entangling his thick fingers in the sides of her panties, and slowly sliding them down her legs. Her pussy throbbed in anticipation. She playfully kicked them to the side, bracing herself for what would come next. Diego began at the inside of her knees, trailing kisses up the sides of her thighs and switching between the two. When his mouth was just about to reach her most sacred parts, he paused again, taking in a slow deep breath.

"Diego, I need you," she whispered.

"I know, baby, but first, let me taste you."

His words echoed through her, and she had never felt more connected to anyone before, as she did at that moment. Diego started to feast on her hot, wet heat, and her breath hitched in her chest. Campbell couldn't hold back as she let out a loud moan, and they just kept coming. Her knees were getting weak. She didn't think she could take much more as she burst into ecstasy while cumming in his mouth. Diego stood and wrapped an arm around her before her knees gave out. He lifted her with ease and pressed her back against the door. He kissed along her neck and up to her lips before he eased back and pulled her away from the doorframe. She looked at him.

"What's wrong?"

He shook his head. "Our first time together is not going to be me taking you up against a door."

He gripped her hips as he carried her up the stairs and into his bedroom.

She glanced around. "So, this is what it looks like in here," she said, and Diego cocked his head sideways.

"You mean you never snooped when I wasn't home?"

She pulled her head back as if she had been insulted. "No. I respect people's privacy."

He grinned before playfully tossing her onto his king-sized bed, and she giggled.

He slipped his jeans off before climbing on the bed and covering her with his body. The skin-to-skin contact between their bodies felt amazing. With one thigh positioned between her legs, he hovered over her and stared into her eyes. Using his thumb, he lightly swiped over her nipple, and she gasped. She reached for his face and cupped his cheeks.

"Diego, please, I need you," she begged.

He lifted his head and grinned at her before lifting his body and positioning himself between her thighs. She reached around and ran her nails up and down his back and rocked her hips. Each time her pussy grazed his cock, he swore it got harder. If he didn't get inside her, he was going to blow his load.

He leaned down and kissed her, nudging his cock slowly into her and pulling out, helping to stretch her sensitive tissues.

Her hands felt incredible as she ran them over his head then down his shoulders. In one thrust, he seated himself fully inside her. She moaned and threw her head back as her hips moved in sync with his.

"Oh, God, Diego. I need more, please…" she begged him.

He sat up a little and gripped her hips, hoping like hell he wouldn't leave finger marks as he pumped his hips faster and harder. He felt the tingling sensation going down his spine straight to his balls. He felt her tighten around him and knew that she was close. Her nails dug into his shoulders and she moaned in ecstasy as she shook and came, and he soon followed, releasing himself inside her.

As he collapsed, he rolled to the side, taking her with him. She curled into him as she panted to catch her breath.

"Goddamn, I love you," he told her as he kissed her head.

She looked up at him with a glowing smile on her face. "I love you too."

He gently caressed her cheek. "You're an amazing woman, and for once in my career, I'll admit that I'm damn glad I got knocked in the fucking head."

"Diego!" She scolded. "That isn't funny. You could've been seriously hurt".

"Maybe. But if I hadn't, I most likely would've never met you. And that would've been a shame because, as Alex told me today, you're my other half."

Campbell snuggled into Diego's side. She caressed his bare chest. Her fingers glided over his taut muscles and the little bit of chest hair he had.

Diego was a gentleman even in bed. Mitchell would have just taken her any way he wanted. There was no asking or caring about her feelings. It was all about him finding his release and satisfaction. She was just a toy to manipulate.

But she didn't have to worry about that anymore. She found a man who loved her for who she was and treated her with dignity and respect.

"Do you ever get scared when you leave for a mission?" She asked, and he stared at her before shaking his head.

"If I did, then I wouldn't be able to perform my job to the fullest. In our line of work, the slightest hesitation could mean life or death for either myself or one of my teammates."

She seemed to process that.

"Are you all taught that during training?"

"I wouldn't say *taught*. It's just the way it is. Many people think being a SEAL is about being the fittest and strongest. But in reality, it's mainly a mental game. You can be the strongest man out there, but if you don't have the mentality to push through what's thrown at you, then ninety-nine percent of the time, you'll quit. BUD/S is not for the weak."

"Hmm...I never knew that."

Diego rolled over onto his side so that he faced her.

"Does me being a SEAL scare you?"

"A little. I'll always worry about you. But listening to you speak about your career and seeing the camaraderie between the team, I understand how important it is for you."

He gave her a serious expression. "It is important to me, but so are you."

She smiled. "I love you."

"I love you, too. Now come here so I can show you how much," he said as he rolled to his back and took her with him. She sat on top of him and looked down. She was in awe of the man he was. Even though the worry was still there in the back of her mind, she remembered the new motto she lived by—to live in the moment. And at this precise moment, she had her man to love.

CHAPTER TWENTY

A few days had passed, and Campbell found herself in a familiar situation. She was alone in the house. The day after Diego regained his active-duty status, the team had been called out. Diego had explained that it was expected, but now that he was physically gone and out of contact, she'd been a nervous Nelly.

She tried keeping herself busy by putting together the furniture that had been delivered for the upstairs bedrooms, but she even found that task hard to concentrate on. She had cleaned the entire house from top to bottom—not that it was dirty—but to try and take her mind off the worrying.

With Diego's departure, he had been worried about who'd look after her in his absence. Even though Derek's friend Tink said that it appeared that Mitchell had left the country, she still wasn't confident in letting down her guard, and neither were the guys.

Every night since Diego left, either Derek or Tink came by to visit and made sure she was okay. Alex came and stayed the first night with her. She had enjoyed the company, and Alex explained some things to her that helped ease her worry a tad. She'd admit that she did cry. Other days, some of the other ladies visited her or called to check on her. Having them to lean on had been a lifesaver.

She looked down at her watch, and her eyes almost bugged out of her head when she saw the time. She only had an hour before she needed to get to work. That was another thing, the day Diego left; she decided she needed to find a job. She didn't see anything wrong with it as most of the other ladies within the team had careers. However, she wouldn't consider her new job a career, per se.

When she saw the job advertisement seeking a professional hostess for a VIP club and had applied for the position, she hadn't realized it was an upscale gentlemen's club until she was called later that afternoon by the owner asking her to come in for an interview.

When she first met Lance, the owner, she apologized and tried to tell him that she was new in town and wasn't aware of the type of club it was. But then Lance asked her to hear him out, and that he was desperate for a hostess for the VIP Club rooms where the private parties were held. She still wasn't convinced because she'd heard about places like that and the shenanigans that go on, especially in the private back rooms.

When he had taken her out into the club itself, it wasn't what she expected to find. She pictured a dark, seedy bar with scantily dressed women swinging around on a pole. But surprisingly, it was the opposite. The main room was well-lit and featured a lot of modern décor and furnishings. Lance also told her that the club did not offer full nudity, and that he wanted a place that featured classy entertainment.

When he explained what the hostess job entailed, she realized it was nothing she hadn't done before when she hosted Mitchell's parties. At least here, she'd earn some serious cash if what Lance told her was true. He said that the previous hostess brought in anywhere from five hundred dollars to sometimes over a grand in one night in tips. Of course, that depended on how many parties she had and the size of them. There was one other woman, Rachel, whom she would be sharing hostess duties with. And between the two of them, they would rotate shifts.

Lance had laughed at her when she asked if being a hostess was all she was required to do to bring in that type of money. She wasn't down for performing any sexual acts. He had assured her that those types of things were not permitted in his club, and if he ever found out that it was, those employees would be fired on the spot.

She was still a little hesitant about it, but she accepted the position on a trial basis until she could find something else, though she hadn't told anyone yet. She first wanted to talk to Diego, but she might be forced to let the others know, not knowing when he would return.

She walked to her and Diego's bedroom and looked at the uniform she'd be wearing for the evening. Lance had told her that most of the waitstaff wore short skirts, but when she told him about her leg and how she was self-conscious about it, he offered an alternative. It was a pair of black dress pants that formed to her hips and thighs. The shirt was a white button-up dress shirt, though the top three buttons were conveniently missing, leaving the V in the top open for her cleavage to show. She got it. Looking sexy was what brought in the tips. But Lance was right; once she had the uniform on, including the black heels, she felt classy but sexy.

Eight hours later, and with sore feet, Campbell thought she was going to collapse. She learned quickly that it was a very popular club. She hardly had a chance to take a break. Lance had partnered her with Rachel so she could get a feel of what was expected. Rachel was friendly and very resourceful. The job itself wasn't hard, it just involved a lot of standing and walking.

As she sat at the little table where the waitstaff gathered at the end of the night to count out their tips, she couldn't help but feel happy inside. Even splitting the tips fifty-fifty with Rachel, she still pocketed a little over four hundred dollars. That was off three parties.

Two of the parties had been great to work with and caused no problems. One was a retirement party, and the other was a going-away party. The third party, however, she could've done without. But in this type of business, she knew she'd be dealing with all sorts of people. But this particular group of guys didn't know when to quit. They were older and got so obnoxious and handsy, trying to feel both her and Rachel up that Rachel had to get the bouncer involved. Even when the bouncer threatened to have them removed, they continued their childish behavior. That was when Lance got involved and told them they were no longer welcome in the club. A few of the guys weren't happy and made threats towards Lance and two of the bouncers.

Campbell quickly learned that Lance wasn't a person to mess with. Rachel had told her that he was former Special Forces. But Campbell had to compliment him. He did take care of his staff when it came to their wellbeing and security.

One of the waitresses who had left just a few minutes ago came back inside because she had forgotten something but told everyone that it had started raining. It wasn't just raining when Campbell went to check; it was pouring, and it showed no signs of letting up. That put her in an awkward situation. With Diego gone, Campbell didn't know where he put the spare keys to his other car, so she had taken the bus to work. With the poor weather outside, that would mean she would have to walk almost a quarter of a mile to catch the bus, then another half a mile from the closest stop to the house in the pouring rain. *Shit!*

She was going to have to call someone. The first person that popped into her head was Alex. She pulled on her big girl panties and tried calling her first. She felt bad for waking her up but then explained the situation to her. She was shocked when Alex laughed when she told her where she was working. But without any hesitation, Alex said to her that she'd be right there that she only lived about ten minutes away.

As she waited by the door, Lance came over to talk with her.

"How was it tonight?" He asked.

"It was good. Besides that one group with the unruly men, everything was great."

He smiled. "Good. So, I'll see you this weekend?"

"I'll be here." At least, she hoped. Again, that all depended on if Diego made it home, and what he thought about her working at a gentlemen's club.

Campbell saw Alex's Escalade pull into the parking lot, and she started walking. The rain had let up a little bit, but not much.

As she made it to the middle of the parking lot, she turned when she heard someone whistle at her. When she looked, she recognized it was the three guys from the party who had given her and Rachel a hard time. Alex must've seen them because she got out of the vehicle and met her halfway.

"Don't even look at them," Alex said with a serious expression. "Just keep walking."

"Hey, sweet thing, who's your friend?" She heard one of them say.

"Friends of yours?" Alex asked as they walked faster.

"No, they were harassing the other hostess and me earlier, and the owner kicked them out."

"Hey, don't run off now. We've been waiting for you. There are plenty of us to keep you ladies company." Another guy shouted, and Campbell could tell the men were following them.

"Oh God," Campbell said, gripping Alex's hand tighter.

"Just keep walking and don't look back," Alex told her calmly, and Campbell wondered how Alex could be so calm and collected.

They only made it a few steps beyond where the guys were standing when one of them lunged toward them and shoved Alex, immediately grabbing Campbell's arm.

"I'll keep this one busy," one of the guys said as he held Alex from behind.

The guy holding Campbell started pulling her towards a big truck, and she began to panic. She heard Alex yelling at the other two guys to let her go. She tried looking over her shoulder, but the way the guy was holding her, she couldn't see.

"You and I are going to have fun getting to know one another. I've been watching you all night." He ran his nose up the side of her neck then licked her ear.

She couldn't let him get her inside that truck. She was shaking because she knew there was no way she could overpower the large guy dragging her across the parking lot, but she could try and slow him down and hope someone inside heard the commotion and would come outside.

Without another thought, she dug her heels into the pavement, but the guy gripped her arm tighter. "Move it bitch. I ain't got time for games."

Suddenly, she heard one of the guys cry out in pain.

"What the hell?" The guy holding her said as he turned around to see what was going on.

That was when Campbell was able to see Alex beating the shit out of the two guys. One guy she kicked in the stomach, and the other who tried to grab her from behind she head butted—blood quickly splattering everywhere as she broke his nose.

The first guy fell to his knees and held his stomach, but then quickly returned to his feet and charged at Alex again. He swung his arm to punch her, but Alex ducked just in time. When popped she countered with a punch of her own and nailed the guy in the eye before striking him in the gut with her elbow.

The guy holding Campbell was so focused on what was happening between Alex and the two guys that Campbell decided to make her move. She took her foot and stomped on his foot with the spiked heel of her shoe. The guy released her, and Campbell started to run toward Alex. But with her limp, she wasn't very fast, and the guy caught her easily. He pulled her backward by her shirt, ripping it in the process. Her heel caught on the pavement, and she fell to the ground. She landed on her hip and felt the ache.

"Get up bitch," he told her, but then Alex was by her side.

"Leave her alone," Alex told him, and the guy turned to face Alex.

The guy took a swing at Alex and struck her in the mouth. But Alex didn't go down, it just seemed to infuriate her as she dished out punch after punch, striking the guy in the face and stomach until he fell to the ground.

Suddenly, the door burst open, and Lance and the two bouncers came running out. "What the hell is going on," Lance asked as he knelt next to Campbell and the bouncers took care of the men.

Campbell heard the sirens in the distance. She looked at Alex, who joined Lance at her side. That was when she noticed that Alex had a busted lip.

"Alex, I'm so sorry."

Alex rushed to calm her down. "It's okay, Campbell. Let's focus on you. You took a pretty bad fall."

"What happened?" Lance asked, and Alex explained about the guys waiting for Campbell.

"Shit! I'm so sorry, Campbell. Had I known they were out here, I would've had Darren or Curtis escort you out. I didn't see anything until you guys came into view on the cameras."

Lance looked toward Alex. "Where in the hell did you learn to fight like that?"

Alex shrugged her shoulders. "SEALs."

A knowing expression crossed his face, and he nodded in understanding.

Seconds later, the parking lot became chaos as it quickly filled with police vehicles and ambulances.

With Alex and Lance's help, they helped Campbell stand up. She was in a little bit of pain, but it was tolerable. Alex asked her if she was okay when suddenly her eyes widened as she stared over her shoulder.

"Oh no."

"What?"

"Don't freak out, but the calvary just arrived."

Diego was eager to get home and see Campbell. Thankfully their mission went off as it was practiced and planned, and the crisis had been averted. Though had they arrived fifteen minutes later, they could've been looking at a possible hostage situation. But that didn't happen—everyone was safe, and that was all that mattered.

He had told Ace, Potter, Stitch, and Irish that he'd give them a lift home since they hadn't had their vehicles.

"What the hell is going on up there?" Potter asked, pointing to all the police activity up ahead.

"Is that Lance's club?" Irish asked, and Stitch agreed that it was.

As they got closer, it appeared to be a serious situation.

Suddenly Ace shouted. "What the fuck! That's Alex's Escalade."

When Diego looked, sure as shit, it was, and he pulled into the parking lot behind one of the police cars. Being that Alex was potentially involved, they all jumped out to see what was going on.

They found Alex first, and she looked shocked to see them. But when the woman standing in front of Alex turned around, Diego felt his jaw hit the ground.

As soon as Campbell locked gazes with Diego, she felt the tears emerge, and she didn't hesitate. She ran as fast as she could to him, seeking his comfort and protection. As soon as she felt his strong arms embrace her, she let loose and began to cry.

She heard Ace fussing over Alex as she was trying to explain what happened. Campbell could hear the anger in Ace's tone, and she didn't want Ace upset with Alex. This was all her doing, and she began to feel awful and responsible. As she eased back from Diego's hold, she looked up, and the fire and intensity in Diego's eyes should've frightened her.

She turned toward Ace, who was now hugging Alex.

"Please don't be upset with Alex. I'm the one who called her. It's my fault. I'm so sorry."

She was in such a tizzy, she didn't even know who put a jacket around her shoulders, but she was thankful for it since her shirt was ripped and her bra was showing, not to mention with all the rain, the shirt was soaked and completely see-through.

Lance then walked up and made sure that both Alex and Campbell were okay. When Irish asked what happened, he reiterated what Alex had told them, though he elaborated more on Alex's role and how she possibly saved both herself and Campbell.

Diego looked at her, then shook his head as if not understanding.

"You work here?" He asked, and Campbell nodded her head.

"Since when?"

"Since today." She started to explain why and how she got the job, but Diego silenced her when he pulled her into a hug. She could feel his body shaking, and she prayed it wasn't out of anger.

"Jesus, I think you just took ten years off my life, woman."

He pulled back and looked down at her. "You and I are going to have a very long discussion when we get home."

"I'm sorry."

He hugged her again. "It's okay. All that matters is that you're okay."

She hugged him back. "Can we go home now?"

"Of course, baby."

Alex sat in the passenger seat, wondering what was going through Ace's head as he drove her car back to their house.

She rubbed her hands on her thighs, debating if she should say anything or just let it be. She knew that eventually, he'd say something about the evening's ordeal.

She closed her eyes for a few minutes and kept thinking if she should've done anything differently, but she kept coming up empty-handed.

She felt the vehicle stop, and her eyes popped open when his large hand landed on her thigh. She looked over at him. He was watching her with his piercing blue eyes that first drew her to him.

"Are you okay?" He asked her. It wasn't a surprise question. Alex knew how much Ace cared for her.

"I've never lied to you, and I won't start now. My lip is a little sore, but it'll heal."

He reached across the console and gently caressed her lip with his thumb. "I don't like seeing you hurt." He blew out a big breath. "I can't believe I'm saying this, but I'm glad you were there. I could only imagine the situation that Campbell would be in right now if you weren't."

"Me too."

"I love you, Alex. You're my world."

She smiled. "I love you, too."

As he started to drive again Alex kept an eye on him. For the past few weeks—and even tonight—he seemed different. She couldn't quite put her finger on what it was, though. But give her enough time, and she'd figure it out.

Campbell stood under the warm spray of water in the large walk-in shower. The slight chill in the nighttime air mixed with her being out in the pouring rain; she felt cold down to her bones.

With her eyes closed, she took a deep breath as she slowly regained the warmth in her body.

Diego hadn't said a word the entire ride home, and she feared the worst. Between the darkness in the truck and his ability to mask his feelings and expressions, she wasn't sure what he was thinking, and that scared her—the unknown completely freaked her out.

Once they had gotten inside the house, he disappeared inside his office. She waited for a few minutes, but when he never emerged, she decided just to head upstairs and take a shower.

When she peeled her slacks off, she saw a bruise had already formed on her hip, along with a few on her arms where the guy had grabbed her. She felt so many emotions; embarrassed, guilty, nervous, and scared.

It felt like an eternity before she heard any sign of Diego, until she felt his large hands sweep over her shoulders, making her body shudder.

She tried to turn around, but he stopped her.

"Don't move," he ordered, and the deep command caused a shiver to run down her spine.

His hands continued down her back, then back up, tracing her spine. Now and then, he'd use his thumbs for kneading the tight muscles in her shoulder blades.

He pressed his body up against her back as he wrapped an arm around her waist. His chin rested on her shoulder, and she could feel his warm breath against her neck.

"Diego..." she said in a breathless voice. His hands felt amazing as they caressed her body.

"Tell me why, Campbell."

She closed her eyes again and took another deep breath. Honesty—she'd give him the truth.

"I needed a job, and that happened to be a position that I had experience in. Diego, I wasn't working in the main club." She rushed to assure him.

"It put you in danger, not to mention, did you ever think that if Mitchell has people out there looking for you that they could've traced a paycheck back to you?"

Oh damn! That she hadn't thought of.

She turned and looked up at him. "I'm sorry. I don't know what else to say except that I'm sorry."

He turned her around and pulled her into a hug, and she wrapped her arms around his waist.

"When I saw you standing there, I didn't know what to think. But it scared me."

She eased back, reached up, and cupped his cheeks. His brown eyes displayed so many emotions.

"Let me show you how sorry I am."

He shook his head, and immediately she began to feel rejected, but then he lifted her into the air, and she straddled his waist.

"There's nothing to forgive. You're human, Campbell. All that matters is that you're safe. Although these bruises you have piss me off."

"I love you," she said.

"I love you too. But right now, you better hold on because it's about to get a little wild in here. I need to be inside you."

She smirked. "Then take me."

CHAPTER TWENTY-ONE

Campbell sat at the kitchen table, making a grocery list. With Diego back in town, she needed to pick up some things for dinners she had planned for the week.

Her morning had started out with a phone call to Lance telling him that she wouldn't be returning to the club. He understood fully but said to her that he would miss her and that she had a job waiting for her if she ever changed her mind. She appreciated it, but she knew Diego would never allow it.

Diego walked into the kitchen and kissed her before grabbing a cup of coffee. After a couple of rounds in the sheets last night—or should she say this morning—she had fallen asleep in Diego's arms, and that was where she woke up.

"What's on the agenda for today?" He asked.

"Well, I need to go to the grocery store. Then I really don't have anything planned. Why? Is there anything you needed to do?"

He shook his head. "No. But Ace just called and invited us over for a barbecue."

She stared at Diego. "He did?" She thought after last night that Ace wouldn't want her anywhere around him or Alex.

"Yeah. The whole team is going to be there."

Well, that made all the difference in the world. If the whole team were invited, it would be a little obvious if they hadn't asked her. Maybe she'd tell Diego it was best if she didn't go.

As if reading her mind, he walked over to the table and sat down next to her.

"Hey, what's the long look for?"

"Nothing," she lied and continued to jot down more items on her list.

Diego's hand covered hers. "Campbell?"

She took a deep breath before looking up and meeting his eyes.

"What's wrong?" He asked.

She started to shake her head, but he stopped her. "Don't do that."

"Do what?" She retorted.

"Don't lie. I can tell something's bothering you. You were fine until I told you about going over to Ace and Alex's house."

She set the pen in her hand down.

"Because I don't think that either Ace or Alex would want me there."

Diego jerked his back. "What? Why would you think that?"

"Because of last night."

His expression softened. "Babe, neither one blame you for last night."

Her eyes widened. "They don't?"

He grinned. "No. Sure, Ace was pissed, but that was because Alex got a busted lip."

"And again, that wouldn't have happened if I hadn't called her."

Diego scooted his chair closer and put his hands over both of hers that were clasped together and resting on the table.

"Ace and I talked, and we both agreed that the situation would've been a hell of a lot worse if Alex hadn't been there. Campbell, those men most likely would've gotten you into their truck. Now the only thing I don't like is that now I have to buy some outrageous thank you gift for Alex."

He grinned, and she realized he was only teasing.

"So, they really don't hate me?"

"Hate you? No. Worried about you? Yes." Diego leaned closer. "Campbell, you need to realize that you being with me solidifies that you're unofficially part of the team. Just as Alex, Tenley, Autumn, Bailey, Mia, Arianna, and Anna Grace are. And like the others have said, it isn't just a team; we're a family. We care about one another and are always there to help one another when things get tough—just like Alex was there for you last night. And I could bet my ass that she'd do it again in a heartbeat if it warranted."

"I understand. I've just never been a part of anything so dynamic."

He smiled. "Well, get used to it, beautiful." He leaned forward and kissed her lips. "Now, come on, let's head to the store. I told Ace I'd pick up the hot dogs and burgers."

Campbell sat outside on the patio at Ace and Alex's house. It turned out to be another gorgeous day. The kids were in the pool with the dogs.

"So, Campbell, how mad was Diego last night?" Bailey asked.

She scrunched her nose up. "Surprisingly, he wasn't. Just worried, and I think I scared him."

"As long as I've been around these types of men, there is only one thing that scares them. And that is when someone close to them is in danger or hurt." Alex told them, and Campbell couldn't stop herself as she glanced at the scab on her lip.

"Alex, I'm so sorry about last night. If I knew—"

Alex cut her off. "Campbell, stop apologizing. Nobody could've predicted what those assholes were up to. God, even Lance called Ace this morning apologizing."

Campbell grinned. "It really is a shame, because Lance seems like a great employer to work for."

"Lance is a badass," Bailey interjected. "I met him one night when I was with Irish."

"Well, either way, my days as a hostess are over," Campbell said.

"Not necessarily," Arianna said, speaking up.

Campbell looked over at her. "What does that mean?"

Arianna glanced around at the others, who all had grins on their faces as if they knew what Arianna was about to share.

"I have a proposition for you."

Campbell tilted her head sideways. "What kind of proposition?"

"Remember at Frost and Autumn's baby shower you asked me about that empty room that sat behind the main room?"

"Yeah?"

"Well, I considered your ideas, ran some numbers, and then ran it by my dad. When I showed him the potential profit he could make by renting that room out, he loved the idea."

Campbell smiled. "That's great, Arianna; as I said, there's so much potential for that room since it's like a blank canvas. You can bring anyone's imagination to life just off their theme. Or you could host theme nights; the list of ideas could go on. That's very exciting."

Arianna smiled wide. "I'm glad you're so excited, because my dad and I would like to offer you the job of Bayside's new event hostess."

Campbell covered her mouth. "You're joking."

Still smiling Arianna, shook her head. "My dad was very impressed with your ideas. You've got a special talent, especially with your creative mind."

"Wow! I don't know what to say." Campbell said, still in shock over the news.

"Say that you'll say yes!"

Campbell grinned. "Of course, I'll say yes. Oh my gosh! I can't believe this. Thank you, Arianna."

"No thanks needed. You earned it. I can't wait to see what you come up with. And be ready come Monday, because my dad already mentioned you to a couple of his friends, and they already want to book events."

Alex lifted her drink into the air. "This calls for a toast. To Campbell and her new endeavor."

"To Campbell!" The others chanted, and Campbell couldn't stop smiling. She couldn't believe how everything was falling into place. When one door closes, another one opens. For the first time in her adult life, she actually had true friends. Not the fake friends she knew and associated with from her dance social circle, but honest to goodness true friends. It was precisely how Diego described it; they were family.

Between all the good that had occurred over the last couple of weeks—a new incredible job that she would be starting in a few days, her freedom, her new amazing friends, and the most remarkable man she had ever met, Diego. Campbell couldn't stop smiling. In fact, she didn't think that anything could erase it.

They were driving to the hardware store in Diego's truck to pick up a few items Diego needed for the house. As they pulled into the parking lot, Campbell felt her phone vibrate in her purse, but there was no incoming call when she pulled it out. She felt the vibration again in her purse, and suddenly, she felt as if her heart stopped beating. There was only one person at least who was still alive that had that number. She reached into her purse, and when she pulled the other phone out, she almost burst into tears when she saw Lizzy's name flash across the screen.

She scrambled to answer it, fearing that she would miss the call.

"Hello?" She answered.

All she got in return was silence. But she knew someone was on the other end because she could hear them breathing.

"Hello?" She repeated, then held her breath.

"Campbell?" The faint voice said from the other side.

Just the sound of her sister's voice had her reaching for Diego's hand, looking for support.

"Lizzy? Is that you?" She asked, and Diego's eyes widened when he heard that and understood what was going on.

"It's me."

"Where are you?" Campbell asked.

"North Carolina."

"Are you okay?"

"I need help, Campbell. I want to come home."

Campbell felt the hot tears rolling down her face. Diego reached over and unbuckled her seatbelt, and she scooted closer to him.

"I'm not in West Virginia anymore."

"You're not?" She asked, sounding shocked.

"No. I'm in Virginia Beach."

"What are you doing in Virginia Beach?"

"It's a long story. Lizzy, are you hurt?"

"No. I just miss you and want to come home. I want us to be a family again."

God, this was killing her. She'd waited so long to hear her sister's voice again.

"Lizzy, can you hold on for a minute."

Campbell put the phone on mute, looked at Diego, and told him what was going on.

"What do you want to do?" He asked her.

Campbell thought about it. Lizzy was family, and she would never turn her back on her family. Pushing aside their differences, Campbell knew she had to help her.

"Diego, I have to help her. She's my sister, and she's asking for help. That probably took a lot of nerve for her to call me."

"Ask her if she can meet you at Bayside on Saturday. If she needs money to get here, tell her we'll send it to her."

Campbell smiled, then leaned over and kissed his cheek.

"Thank you."

She got back on the phone with Lizzy and made plans for Saturday. After the call and as she and Diego headed inside the store, Campbell suddenly felt a strange sensation as if she was starting to second guess herself. But the worst that could happen was that Lizzy would never show, and they'd be out a few hundred dollars.

"Well, did she buy it? Did she take the bait?"

Lizzy closed the old flip phone and looked at Mitchell.

"She offered to send me money to help me get there if that answers your question. She's in Virginia Beach. I'm supposed to meet her at some place called Bayside on Saturday."

Mitchell felt his stomach fill with excitement. He knew that Belle couldn't hide forever. It was only a matter of time before he located her.

Mitchell looked at Lizzy with disgust as she smacked her lips as she ate the steak dinner he had bought for her. It hadn't taken much to get her to cooperate with him. Just a little bit of cash and some drugs, and she was putty in his hands.

"So, when do I get the money and product you promised me?"

Mitchell gritted his teeth and tried to hide his anger towards the little bitch. Belle always talked about how selfish her sister was, and he saw it first-hand.

"I'll have Vinny drop it off to you at your hotel tomorrow morning."

"Alright. Well, if you don't need anything else from me, I'm going to skedaddle."

She wiped her mouth with her shirt sleeve. When she got up from the table, she nearly fell. She was nothing but a drunk and druggie. How Belle was related to her was mind-boggling.

Once she was gone, Vinny walked over and took the seat next to him.

"That girl is messed up. Are you really going to give her cash and more meth?"

Mitchell looked at Vinny as if he was crazy.

"Hell no."

"What are you going to do then?"

Mitchell stared at Vinny. "You know what to do."

Vinny gave him a wicked grin. "Yes, sir."

"And make it quick because we have a plane to catch in two days. I've got a date with my Belle."

Mitchell rubbed his hands together. Soon he'd be reunited with Belle, and they'd be on their way to Russia to their new home. She had a lot of making up to do. He laughed wickedly, thinking that there was no better time than to use the dungeon in the basement of the new mini-castle he purchased not far from the mine.

He picked up his drink and looked at Vinny. "To new beginnings."

CHAPTER TWENTY-TWO

Campbell was feeling anxious about her sister's impending arrival. Lizzy had texted a few minutes ago and told her that she was running late but that she'd be there. In the meantime, and to help keep her mind busy, she went over the final preparations for the big Landry party for tomorrow. They had actually closed the bar and restaurant early so they could prepare. It was a retirement party for a high-ranking Navy officer, and they rented the entire restaurant and bar.

Arianna walked up. "Hey, are you sure your sister is coming?"

"She texted and said she was running a little late. She'll be here."

"Do you want me to hang around until she gets here?"

Campbell smiled. "No. But thank you. I'll be good. I still need to plan the menu for the Berkley party next weekend. They want to see a couple of options before they make a decision."

Arianna eyed her. "Okay…if you're sure."

"Positive."

"Okay, just make sure you lock up behind me. Is Diego picking you up?"

"Not tonight. He called earlier and said that the team was called into some emergency meeting. Whatever that meant."

"Oh, that's right. Dino did send me a text telling me that they were on standby. Well, then, I guess I'll see you tomorrow."

Campbell smiled. "Yes, you will. It's going to be a busy day."

Campbell walked Arianna to the door and relocked it after she left. She walked over to the bar and poured herself a Coke before sitting back down and starting on the menu for next weekend.

Autumn grabbed a pint of *Cookie Two Step* ice cream from the small grocer's freezer. She had been feeling exhausted and laid down after Frost had left to go to the base, but then woke up a little while ago and was having a craving for ice cream. Of course, they had none left in the house because she ate it all. So, she ended up getting in her car and driving up the street to the little corner grocery store that was open twenty-four hours.

As she waited in line to pay, she felt a sharp pain in her back. It was quick, but it hurt like hell. She had some Braxton Hicks contractions a few days ago and had the doctor check her out. She informed Autumn that it was a false alarm and that she hadn't even started to dilate.

When it was her turn at the register, she reached into her purse, and suddenly another pain hit her. This one was a little stronger. She quickly swiped her debit card and paid for the ice cream.

As she walked to her car, another wave of pain zipped right through her. This one made her stop and pause next to the vehicle. She had to catch her breath. Just as she reached for the handle to the door, she felt the trickle of liquid down her legs. Knowing she hadn't peed, it only meant one thing—her water broke.

She grabbed Cody's beach towel he had left in the car and placed it under her as quickly as she could. She had another contraction, and this one was felt in the front. She started to do her breathing exercises to bear the pain. She reached into her purse to get her phone so she could try calling Frost, when she remembered she had left her cell phone charging on the nightstand next to the bed. *Crap!*

She started the car and drove out of the parking lot when another contraction came, and she cringed from the pain. There was no way she was going to make it to the hospital driving herself. She just needed to get back to the house, and she could call Frost or someone to take her.

Just as she was passing Bayside, another contraction hit. She saw Campbell's car was still in the parking lot, and she pulled in. *Thank God.* She grabbed her purse, slid out of the vehicle, and waddled up to the door. She pulled on the handle, but it was locked. "Oh, God, please be in there." She mumbled to herself as she pounded on the door.

Suddenly a face appeared in the window, and she breathed a sigh of relief when she saw it was Campbell.

As soon as Campbell opened the door, Autumn didn't waste any time.

"Baby is coming," she said in between pants as she continued to breathe through the pain. Jesus, she didn't remember having this much pain when she delivered Cody.

"Oh shit!" Campbell blurted out.

Campbell had all but given up on her sister and had started to close down the inside when she heard someone beating on the door. At first, she assumed it was her sister, but she became concerned when she looked out the window and saw Autumn, clearly in some sort of distress. Quickly, she flipped the lock and pulled the door open.

"Autumn?"

"Baby is coming," Autumn said in between heavy breaths.

"Oh shit! Did you try calling Frost?"

"No. My phone is at home. I just wanted ice cream."

Campbell helped Autumn inside and relocked the door behind them. She'd take them out the side door where her car was and call someone else to come to pick up Autumn's car later.

"Come on. I'll drive you to the hospital. Crap, is Cody at home?"

Autumn shook her head as she did her breathing techniques. "No. He's at a friend's house."

On the way out, Campbell grabbed her purse and keys from the office. She got Autumn outside and seated inside the car. As she went to close the door, Autumn looked at her. "Oh no."

"What? What's wrong?" Campbell asked worriedly. She had never dealt with a woman in labor before.

"My water broke, and I'm going to get your seats wet."

"It's fine. Don't worry about it," she said, then slammed the door and ran around to the driver's side.

As she pulled out of the parking lot and started down the road, she never noticed the grey SUV that did a U-turn and started to follow them.

Campbell looked over at Autumn. She was holding her stomach and looked like she was in so much pain. Campbell found herself cringing each time Autumn had a contraction. They were coming faster. She hit Diego's number first, and it went straight to voicemail. She tried Frost's next, and his went to voicemail also. *Dammit!*

Autumn reclined the seat all the way back and rolled to her left side.

"I can breathe a little better like this," she told Campbell, and Campbell just nodded her head.

Suddenly, out of nowhere, bright headlights reflected in the rearview mirror, almost blinding her.

"What the hell?" She said, and Autumn asked what was wrong, but Campbell didn't want to add to Autumn's worries and told her it was nothing.

She kept an eye on the vehicle behind her because the driver would back off, then drive right on her back bumper. There was a red light ahead, and she considered running it, but she wouldn't be careless with Autumn in the car. As she approached the intersection and started to slow down, the vehicle behind her moved slightly to the left, and when the light from an oncoming car shined into the vehicle, she recognized the driver. *Vinny!*

She began to panic. How had he found her? If Vinny was here, that meant that Mitchell was nearby. *Think Campbell!*

It wasn't just about Campbell's safety. She had Autumn and her unborn baby to worry about. She dialed 911. When the dispatcher answered, she explained what was going on. The dispatcher said they were sending help and for her to keep driving. Just as the dispatcher told her that, Vinny bumped the back of the car and almost caused her to fishtail and lose control. She relayed to the dispatcher what happened, but the dispatcher again advised her to keep driving and that the police were minutes away. She didn't have minutes!

When Vinny tapped the back again, Campbell knew she couldn't put Autumn in danger any longer. She remembered there was a park about a mile or two up ahead, and she told the dispatcher she was pulling into there and to send the police and ambulance to that location. The dispatcher was telling her not to do that when Campbell hung up on her.

Campbell stepped on the gas and put some distance in between her and Vinny's vehicle. She turned into the park's entrance and thank the lord that the park didn't have gates. She sped through the winding roads leading back toward the trails. She was looking for a place to hide the car. She could see the headlights from Vinny's car starting to creep up on her again and knew she was running out of time.

She looked down at Autumn and could tell by her face that she was close to delivering her baby. For Autumn's sake, Campbell knew she had to be the calm one. She saw a turn-off just ahead and knew what she had to do.

Campbell made the abrupt turn and pulled the car alongside a large tree. She looked down at Autumn and handed her the phone.

"Autumn, call Alex and let her know what is going on."

"What are you going to do?" Autumn asked, looking worried.

"These guys want me, and your safety comes first. I could never live with myself if something happened to you or your baby. Just stay as quiet as you can and stay down. The police should be here soon. Tell Diego that Mitchell found me. Tell him that I love him."

Campbell opened the door just as she saw the headlights approaching. She looked back at Autumn before she shut the door and prayed she and the baby would be okay.

She walked toward the oncoming vehicle, and it stopped right in front of her. Vinny jumped out and grabbed her arm just as the back door flew open.

"A mountain girl turned beach girl. Who would've suspected that? Get in the fucking car Belle." Mitchell ordered, and Campbell felt his anger all through her body.

Vinny shoved her inside, and Mitchell grabbed her arm and yanked her closer. He didn't waste any time as he grabbed her face and forcefully kissed her. She tasted the alcohol and felt like she wanted to throw up. She tried to pull away, but that just earned her a hit upside the head.

Finally, when he had his fill, he eased back and smirked evilly. "Welcome home, Belle."

As they drove back down the road, she couldn't help but look out the back window where her car sat. She prayed that Autumn would be alright. Just as they turned out of the park and onto the main road, several police vehicles, an ambulance, and a fire truck turned into the entrance to the park.

She closed her eyes, feeling some relief. *Thank God.*

Fred stood inside the medical examiner's room. He had seen and smelled death before back in his days in the military. He tried breathing through his mouth, but it didn't do any good.

He was afraid his worst fear had come true. He had gotten a phone call from a friend of his friend who was the Sheriff in the next town over, and he raced over. They had found a body of a woman who matched Campbell's description. He had already called Derek but couldn't get a hold of him.

The medical examiner stepped up to the table.

"We just need confirmation of the body." Fred nodded his head and readied himself. As the technician pulled the sheet back and the strawberry blonde hair was exposed, his chest tightened to the point he could hardly breathe. As the sheet moved lower, inch by inch, the young woman's bruised and battered face came into view, and Fred couldn't hold back his sob.

"Sir?" The medical examiner asked, and Fred felt Sheriff Franks grasp his shoulder.

"Damn, Fred. Is it her?"

He looked up, wiping his eyes, and shook his head. "No, it's not her, but it's her sister."

He felt like an asshole crying because even though Lizzy had her issues, nobody deserved to be murdered.

Once he got himself composed, he turned back to the Sheriff. "If you're looking for a suspect, start with Mitchell Langford. I can almost guarantee he's responsible for this. The man is manipulative, and most likely, he used this woman to lure out Campbell. He's going after her next."

"Shit. Where's Campbell now?"

"Virginia Beach."

"I'll make some calls."

Fred just prayed that they made it time.

Diego shoved the last of the clothes into the bag he was taking home to wash. He secured his gear locker and headed toward the door with the others when Derek flew out of his office with his phone up to his ear. He whistled for them and waved everyone back.

"Okay, honey. I've got the team right here with me. I'll relay everything you just told me to them." Derek looked at Frost. "Yes, he's still here. We're heading there now."

"What's going on?" Ace asked.

When Derek took a deep breath and appeared to bite his cheek, Diego knew that whatever the commander knew wasn't anything good.

"It's Autumn. She's in labor."

"Shit!" Frost exclaimed and started for the door, but Derek stopped him.

"She's in Campbell's car in the parking lot at Lake Lawson."

"Lake Lawson? I don't understand. What are they doing there?"

"Alex is with her, and an ambulance is there now tending to her."

He took a deep breath and looked at Diego, and Diego swallowed hard.

"Diego, while Campbell was driving Autumn to the hospital, a car tried to run them off the road. According to Autumn, Campbell knew the person. Out of fear of injuring Autumn and the baby, Campbell pulled into the park and gave herself up."

Diego felt as his chest slowly tightened.

"Where is Campbell now?" He asked, but he already knew the answer. He just needed to hear it.

"Mitchell took her."

"Fuck!"

"Alex said that the police are waiting for us, so let's move. On the way, we'll discuss strategy on how we'll get her back."

Fifteen minutes later, they were all standing around Campbell's car. Frost was with Autumn as the paramedics got her ready for transport to the hospital. She hadn't delivered the baby yet, but Diego could see how much pain she was in. He credited her with relaying important information that could help locate Campbell.

"So, what do we do now?" Diego asked.

"Tink's working on something. He said to hang tight." Derek said just before his phone rang. He looked at the screen, then at Diego. "It's Fred."

"Fred?"

"I see. Jesus, that's terrible."

"Yeah. There's no sign of her."

"Will do. Bye."

"What did he want?" Diego asked. He was chomping at the bit to start looking for Campbell. The police had put out an APB on a grey SUV. They were able to get a partial plate from one of the police car's dashcams. Apparently, the police had just missed them as one of the officers remembered seeing a grey SUV pulling out of the park as they were entering.

"They found Campbell's sister. She was murdered."

"Fuck!" Diego blurted out. "Mitchell?" He asked as the anger started to spill over.

"They aren't positive, but considering the location where she was found, most likely. The authorities in West Virginia are looking for him."

Derek's phone rang again, and he answered. It was a quick call, but as soon as he disconnected, he looked at the team minus Frost, who was with Autumn.

"Let's move. Tink's got something."

CHAPTER TWENTY-THREE

The team had gathered their gear and were waiting on orders from Derek. They were yet to be given any specifics. Derek said he was still working some avenues and told them to hang tight for a few minutes.

Diego couldn't stop pacing the room. He was upset with himself. He promised Campbell that he'd always protect her. Ace and others tried to talk to him, giving him some positive words of encouragement, but he just couldn't. Not until Campbell was found safe.

Moments later, Derek walked into the room.

"Do we know where we're headed?" Diego asked.

"He took her to Russia," Derek announced.

"Russia?!" Diego exclaimed.

"Tink was able to make a few calls and got the flight manifest for a private plane registered to Igor Vasiliev that left out of Virginia Beach Airport about an hour and a half ago."

"And Campbell's name was on it?"

"No, but her sister's name was." They all knew that her sister was dead—a victim in this twisted ordeal.

"Shit!"

"At least we have an idea of where they're headed," Derek mentioned.

"Yeah, but Russia is a big fucking country."

"A few of Mitchell's men were detained at the airport, and two of them aren't as loyal to Mitchell as he thought because they're both singing like canaries."

"It appears that when Mitchell sold the mining company in West Virginia, he invested the majority of the profit into a diamond mine in Siberia, Russia."

"Jesus. That's like in no man's land—way the fuck up there." Potter stated.

Derek nodded. "It is. Anyway, that's where we believe he's headed."

"What can we do? Or should I say authorized to do?"

Derek smirked. "Tink is fueling his jet as we speak. We're also in contact with the FBI, and they're assisting."

"So, I have permission to go?" Diego pressed.

"Not just you. We're all going."

Minutes later, everyone boarded the jet and were buckling in when Derek greeted someone at the door.

"I was wondering if you guys were going to make it."

Everyone was shocked when Alex and Frost appeared in the doorway. Diego sought out Ace, and even Ace seemed surprised, especially to see Alex.

"Alex?" Ace questioned.

Before she could speak, Derek jumped in. "She wanted to help. In my opinion, she could be the best asset we have right now, considering she speaks the language."

Diego forgot that Alex was fluent in four other languages besides English, including Russian.

"Frost, we thought you'd be with Autumn," Stitch said as Frost dropped his gear. He had a shit-eating grin on his face.

"Autumn gave birth on the way to the hospital. She and the baby are both doing fine. She forced me here. Believe me, I wanted to stay by their side, but she told me that Campbell had sacrificed herself to save her and our baby, and that Campbell needed all the resources available, so here I am—ready to help bring her home."

"Dude, was it a boy or a girl?" Skittles asked, and Frost grinned.

"A boy."

"Lucky," Potter muttered, but Diego knew deep down Potter loved his girls and wouldn't trade them for the world.

Everyone offered their congratulations. As the plane started to taxi out, Frost took the empty seat next to Diego.

"We're going to find Campbell, and when we do, I'm going to treat her to whatever the hell she wants. If it wasn't for her quick thinking, I don't know if Autumn and baby Aiden would be here."

Diego only nodded his head. He hoped like hell that they found her.

CHAPTER TWENTY-FOUR

Campbell slowly pried her eyes open and tried to focus on her surroundings. The room she was in looked different from the one she was brought to earlier. She turned her head and looked out the window. Even the view was different. The room she remembered being in last was much larger and decorated nicely. It also had a view of the gardens even though it was covered in a blanket of snow.

She shook her head, trying to clear the fuzziness that surrounded her. The last thing she remembered was Mitchell giving her something to drink. He must've put something in it.

She had no clue where they were. When she asked Mitchell when they landed, he never answered. Wherever they were, it was still winter, given the ice and snow on the ground.

She looked around the room. She was sitting on a bed, but the space didn't appear to be a bedroom. It reminded her of a room with a bed for someone to crash in. Maybe it was connected to an office.

Suddenly, the door swung open, and Mitchell walked in.

"Glad to see you're finally awake. I thought I might have given you too much of the sleeping aids."

Campbell wasn't a fan of putting medicine in her body, especially when it wasn't warranted.

"What did you give me?" She asked, still feeling a bit loopy.

"Just a few over-the-counter sleeping aids. Don't worry; they'll wear off in due time. Right now, you and I need to talk. I also believe there's a punishment to be meted out for your behavior."

She tensed up. *No!* She wasn't going to let him punish her again. She couldn't go through that again. She stood and started to slowly back away from him, and he just shook his head and tsked at her.

"Belle, you've upset me immensely."

He stalked toward her and started to remove his belt. Instantly her body began to shake as she recalled the last meeting she had with the strip of leather. She looked down at her covered arms. No, she couldn't endure that again.

"Don't shy away from me, Belle. You know that it will only make your punishment that much harsher. Just accept it. The sooner you do, the sooner you and I can get to our reunion."

He lunged for her, but she scampered away. Her freedom was short-lived when he clutched a large chunk of her hair and dragged her across the room as she screamed at him. He lifted her by her shirt, ripping it in the process before he flung her onto the bed. She tried scrambling to the other side, but he caught her ankle and pulled her back down the bed.

"Don't touch me. I hate you!" She screamed at him and tried to kick him.

"Look, you little bitch, you've caused me nothing but problems over the last few months. I should kill you just like I killed your sister."

Her eyes welled with tears as she looked at him. *Was Lizzy dead?* Sure, their family bond had been broken, but she never wished death upon her sister. In fact, she hoped that Lizzy could crawl out of the hole that held her down.

"She served her purpose. Her time was limited anyway. The amount of drugs she consumes in a day, she was living on borrowed time. I just did her a favor and ended the agony."

Campbell realized it was Lizzy who tipped him off on where she was. Her own sister had manipulated her.

"You are such a hateful person. I hate you!" She shouted.

The backhand was quick, powerful, and one she wasn't expecting. She tumbled off the bed and onto the floor.

He held her by her face in a crushing grip. She stared into his eyes because there was nowhere else to look. He was in control and too powerful of a man to fight. She was scared.

"Just like I know, it was you who turned those documents into the Feds to have me shut down." He gave her a wicked grin. "You of all people should know that I have people everywhere to bail me out."

Then he delivered another blow. "I knew your dad was documenting everything. That's why I had him killed, then staged it to look like an accident."

The tears streamed down her face, and she tried to wipe them away, but they continued to fall.

"Try and find a way out of this place. Because I can guarantee you that you can't, this castle is like a fortress. Plus, you wouldn't survive outside in the elements."

The door to the room opened, and Vinny entered. She looked at him, and all he did was smirk as if he was happy to see her face bruised.

"The car is out front." He told Mitchell, and Mitchell nodded in understanding.

He turned back to Campbell. "Get up. We're going for a short ride."

"Where?" She questioned. She didn't trust him. For all, she knew he was taking her somewhere to kill her.

"To see our new operation."

Vinny grabbed her arm and yanked her up. He walked downstairs and out a side door toward an SUV. It was cold and dreary outside, just like her life was at the moment. She eyed an open field to the right and saw a group of people just beyond that. Suddenly, she got a burst of courage as she remembered the promise she made to herself—she wouldn't become a victim anymore.

As she limped along, she put all her weight behind her as she sidestepped in front of Vinny's legs before ramming her hip into him. He lost his balance and fell to the ground, but he took her with him. She tried to scramble to her feet, but he grabbed her ankle and pulled her back into his grasp. She kicked her other leg and struck him in the face, and he dropped her leg. As he grabbed his face and shouted, she got to her feet and started running toward the field. She heard him yelling and carrying on from behind her and knew he had given chase. She kept looking back as he gained on her.

She heard him growl in frustration as he almost had her. When she went to look back again, something hard struck her in the chest and was so powerful that it sent her flying into the air. She landed on her shoulder and felt the instant pain. It felt as if her bone broke.

When she looked up to see what had hit her, Mitchell was standing over her. He looked so different. She'd seen him mad before, but his expression was malicious.

"Get up, Belle," he commanded

She tried to crawl away, but he kicked her in the side. She screamed and instinctively curled her body into a ball.

"I said, get up." He yelled, and when she didn't oblige, he kicked her again.

She could hear the frustration in his voice, and she knew she had pushed him past his breaking point.

"I've had enough; take her to the pit."

"Please, don't do this." She pleaded with him as Vinny lifted her by her injured arm, and she screamed out in agony as the pain radiated through her entire shoulder area.

"You've left me no choice. You're a liability to me." Mitchell told her.

Vinny walked her over to a large hole that had been recently dug, going by the fresh dirt. She was teetered on the edge of it as she watched Mitchell walk to some sort of wagon that held a bunch of tools. Her eyes widened when he returned carrying a shovel. As he neared where she stood, he swung shovel toward her, but she saw it coming and ducked. But when she did, she lost her footing on the loose dirt and fell backward into the hole. Her body was like a ragdoll as it tumbled down the side. As soon as she hit bottom, her head made contact with a large rock. She tried to focus, but the blow to her head had been too severe. As the blackness clouded her vision, and before she lost consciousness, she thought she heard someone call her name, followed by gunshots.

"Where did they go?" Diego asked the guy again, but he refused to talk.

When they had arrived at the castle with assistance from Igor, they had found two of Mitchell's men there. But they were tight-lipped and not talking.

"I said I don't know," the guys stated arrogantly.

Diego was starting to get pissed and frustrated because he knew they were running out of time.

Potter stepped forward and took hold of the guy's arm and twisted it.

"My friend asked you a question. Now answer him."

The guy looked at Potter. "Fuck off! I ain't telling you nothing, and you can't make me. I got rights."

The guy glanced toward the two FBI agents who were assisting. But to Diego's surprise, they both turned their backs to the guy, and Potter grinned before he twisted the guy's arm and applied more pressure. Diego could see the guy was close to cracking.

"Don't you fucking lie to me, or I'll snap your arm in half," Potter told him.

"Fuck! Stop! Stop! I'll tell you. He said he was taking her to the hole."

"The hole?"

"He just said the hole. That's all I know, man. Please don't break my arm." Potter released him into the custody of the two FBI agents.

"What in the hell is the hole?" Diego asked.

Igor's eyes widened. "Shit!"

Diego looked at him. "What?"

"The pit. He's taking her to the pit."

"What's the pit?"

"It's the new hole we started digging for mining purposes. That has to be the hole the guy was talking about. Come on, I'll get you guys there."

They all filed out and loaded into several SUVs waiting out in front

As they pulled the vehicles on the scene, Igor pointed. "There!"

As Diego looked closer, he realized it was a bulldozer pushing dirt into the hole.

"There's Mitchell," Igor stated and pointed to a guy running from the scene. Just as Diego thought the fucker would escape again, a police car intercepted him. Mitchell had a death wish because he reached into his jacket and pulled a black pistol out. Multiple shots were fired, and they watched as Mitchell's lifeless body fell to the ground.

The sound of the bulldozer pulled Diego back into action. He leaped out of the vehicle and ran towards the machine. He climbed the bulldozer and punched the guy operating it in the head and knocked him out. Before he turned it off, he put it in reverse and backed it away from the edge. Once he was sure that it was at a far enough distance, he turned the engine off and threw the key out onto the ground.

As he climbed down, he heard Stitch call for a medic. He peered over the edge and looked down into the small crater and saw Campbell lying unresponsive at the bottom, half-covered with dirt.

Not waiting for direction, Diego descended into the hole against recommendations not to until they could assess the stability of the pit. If it caved in, then it was going to swallow both of them—but damn if he was going to leave her down there by herself.

Once he reached the bottom and made it to Campbell, he knew instantly that the situation was dire. She needed medical help pronto. More sirens could be heard in the distance, but Diego wondered if it was too late.

He felt dirt falling, and when he looked up, he saw Stitch making his way down into the hole.

"Stitch, you shouldn't be here," Diego told him. He didn't want any of the others to endanger themselves.

"We don't leave teammates behind." Stitch reminded him.

Stitch started to assess Campbell's injuries.

"It doesn't help that it's fucking freezing out, and she's not dressed for the weather. She must've hit her head on that rock." Stitch felt for her pulse, and his expression turned grim. "Her pulse is weak."

Diego looked at her. Her beautiful skin was covered in bruises and cuts. Her shoulder even looked out of place, and he wondered if she had broken it when she fell. He gritted his teeth and was thrilled that the fucker was dead.

Soon the paramedics arrived, and they took over treating Campbell. Within minutes they had her strapped to a backboard and were carefully lifting her out of the pit.

By the time Diego and Stitch were pulled out, the medics had already loaded Campbell into the back of the ambulance and were headed down the road.

Ace gripped his shoulder. "Come on, let's head to the hospital."

CHAPTER TWENTY-FIVE

Campbell rolled over in bed and looked at the time on the clock next to the bed. When she had come upstairs to lie down for a little bit, she hadn't meant to sleep the whole afternoon away.

She was still dealing with some side effects from her injuries, mainly the head injury she sustained from hitting the rock when she fell inside the pit. She had been a mess when she had woken up in the hospital in Russia. Besides the concussion, she had a dislocated shoulder, which they corrected in the hospital, and thank goodness she had been unconscious when they put it back in place. She had heard from others that it was a painful experience. Besides the many cuts and bruises, she still experienced some double and blurred vision now and then, along with some major headaches. She had spent an entire week in the hospital before she was released. And once she returned home to her and Diego's house, she had slept that following week, except for the constant waking she endured because of the concussion.

Today would be the first day she'd seen her friends since she had come home. Diego invited everyone over for a barbecue. Alex had offered to host it at her and Ace's house, but Diego thought it would be easier on her if they held it at their house. She couldn't wait to see everyone, including the newest addition to Team 2—baby Aiden.

If Mitchell hadn't been killed, he would've been facing life in prison for the many heinous crimes he had committed over the years, which included multiple counts of murder. Two of those charges were her dad and her sister.

The last few days had been a little emotional. With assistance from Fred and Stella, she made sure that her sister received a proper burial next to her parents. Diego promised that one day, once she was up for traveling, he'd take her up to West Virginia to pay her respects.

She felt the bed dip and knew Diego had joined her. As she rolled over, she was met by those dark chocolate eyes that she adored. Diego had been her rock over the last few weeks. He hadn't left her side since the incident. She knew it was difficult for him to watch as her body slowly healed, and she didn't miss the fierce look in his eyes every time her bruises were visible.

She smiled as she curled into his large body. He kissed the top of her head.

"How are you feeling?" He asked her.

"Good. My nap helped." She knew everyone would be arriving soon, but she was content at the moment. She eased her head back and looked at him.

"I love you."

He gave her that sexy smile she had grown fond of. "I love you, too. In fact, I fall more in love with you every day." He sat up, and she followed. He took her hands and brought them to his lips. "You caught my eye the moment you delivered my breakfast that day at the diner. I was attracted to your beauty, elegance, and personality." He reached into the pocket of his jeans and pulled out a diamond ring. It was a Semi-Bezel setting with a single classic solitaire diamond. He took her left hand into his. "I only have one life, and I want to live it with you, Campbell. Say you'll marry me."

A tear slipped out of her eye, and she sniffled. "You'll always be my number one."

He raised his eyebrows. "Is that a yes?"

She smiled and nodded her head. "Yes. It's a definite yes. I'll marry you."

He slid the white gold ring onto her finger before he gathered her into his arms. "I love you so much." He told her before he kissed her gently, being careful with her bruises.

When she pulled back, she grinned up at him with tear-filled eyes. "I love you, too."

All of a sudden, he leaped off the bed and opened the bedroom door.

"She said yes!" He shouted, and all she heard were the cheers and congratulations coming from downstairs.

She looked at him and smiled. "Is everyone already here?"

He grinned. "Yeah. I wanted all our friends to celebrate with us."

She pushed the covers off her legs and slowly got to her feet. She walked over to where her future husband stood and hugged him. "I wouldn't want it any other way."

He took her hand and led her out of the bedroom toward the stairs. As they went to join their friends and family, Diego looked at her.

"I'm warning you now; Alex is already in planning mode."

"Planning mode?"

"Our wedding."

Campbell laughed as they descended the stairs. She had heard all about Alex's weddings, and secretly she couldn't wait either. But until then, she would cherish the moments as they came, and find happiness and comfort in Diego's arms.

EPILOGUE

Ace smiled as he looked on, witnessing the last of his teammates take the plunge into marital bliss. Diego and Campbell deserved all the happiness that life could bring them.

He scanned the beautifully decorated patio where the reception was taking place. When the woman he was seeking emerged from the French doors on the upper deck, he felt his heart skip a beat.

It was hard for him to believe that just two years ago to the month, on a hunt to capture a terrorist, he had met the woman that he planned to spend the rest of his life with. Though their initial meeting had been unexpected and brief, the pint-sized dynamo had barreled into his life like a force to be reckoned with.

Alex Hardesty was an extraordinary woman with many talents. She turned heads wherever she went. And it wasn't just because of her stark beauty and intelligent mind. Alex was filled with compassion, class, and not to mention she was a badass operative.

Alex had stolen his heart right there in the sands of Afghanistan. Together, they became one unit and took charge in making sure that their team's family was looked after.

Life was perfect for the two of them, but there was one important thing missing—a wedding band on her finger.

Alex deserved her happily ever after, and Ace would see to it that she got it.

A Trident Wedding is available now!

BOOK LIST

The Trident Series
ACE
POTTER
FROST
IRISH
STITCH
DINO
SKITTLES
DIEGO
A TRIDENT WEDDING

The Trident Series II - BRAVO Team

JOKER
BEAR
DUKE *(2023)*
PLAYBOY *(2023)*
AUSSIE *(2023)*
NAILS *(TBF)*
NAILS *(TBD)*
JAY BIRD *(TBD)*

ABOUT THE AUTHOR

Jaime Lewis, a *USA TODAY* bestselling author, entered the indie author world in June 2020 with ACE, the first book in the Trident Series.

Coming from a military family, she describes as very patriotic; it's no surprise that her books are known for their accurate portrayal of life in the service.

Passionate in her support of the military, veterans, and first responders, Jaime volunteers with the Daytona Division of the US Naval Sea Cadet Corps, a non-profit youth leadership development program sponsored by the U.S. Navy. Together with her son, she also manages a charity organization that supports military personnel and their families, along with veterans and first responders.

Born and raised in Edgewater, Maryland, Jaime now resides in Ormond Beach, Florida with her husband and two very active boys.

Between her day job, her two boys, and writing, she doesn't have a heap of spare time, but if she does, you'll find her somewhere in the outdoors. Jaime is also an avid sports fan.

Follow Jaime:
Facebook Author Page:https://www.facebook.com/jaime.lewis.58152
Jaime's Convoy: https://www.facebook.com/groups/jaimesconvoy
Goodreads: https://www.goodreads.com/author/show/17048191.Jaime_Lewis

Made in the USA
Monee, IL
21 June 2023